Someday

Susan Schmelzer

The towns depicted in this book are real places but all names, characters, and incidents are the

product of the author's imaginations or used fictitiously. Any resemblance to actual events,

business establishments, locales, persons, living or dead is coincidental.

Elizabeth Publication

9800 Roberts Rd. S.E.

Galloway, Ohio 43119

Someday

Grateful acknowledgement to my editor, Frances Asbury Pruitt

ISBN: 978-1-7327595-1-0

Chapter 1

"Dispatch, this is squad 194. We're on the scene. Got a young male driver pinned unconscious in a rollover. Call Air Care."

The firemen worked quickly with the Jaws of Life to extract the driver and put him on a cot. "When's the chopper coming?"

Staticky answer—"In ten minutes."

"Tell them he's not waking up and vitals are unstable."

The firemen watched, monitoring blood pressure. This guy was sagging. "That helicopter better hurry."

***

"Hello?"

"Hello, this is Kate, a nurse from Mercy Medical Center..." Jill sprang up from a sleepy state of mind with a gasp.

The nurse continued. "We have a young male who is being admitted without any I.D. The firefighters were able to pull him out of the vehicle unconscious, with a cell phone showing a text to this number."

Jill burst into tears and panicked! "Is it Travis? Travis Gunner?"

Kate responded, "Ma'am, we don't know who he is. We're hoping you could tell us. The cell phone is either frozen-up or broken. Firemen are still working to remove the passenger's side door to see if there is any identification in the glove box. Could you come to the hospital to identify him?"

Jill was out of bed, tossing on her jeans, "Um...yes! No! I mean I can get my roommate to come until I can get there. I'm in Chicago."

"That would be great. Have her come to the emergency desk at Mercy Medical Center, and ask for me. My name is Kate."

Jill began to shake as she grabbed her makeup bag and pulled her hair up into a ponytail while trying to hold her phone with her shoulder, "Is he going to live?"

"He's in and out of consciousness, but he's at the best hospital with the best doctors." Then, hearing Jill's sob, she added with compassion, "Miss, if you could send a prayer up for him it would be good."

Jill tried to pull herself together to speak but could only whimper. "Yes, yes I will. Thank you." Before she hung up she asked the nurse, "Can you please call me if you hear any more news about him?"

"Yes, ma'am, I will. Take care and get here safely."

"Yes, okay I will. Thank you."

The last time Jill had talked to Travis it didn't end well. He was hurt and disappointed about her acceptance of a travel position for the summer without considering the plans they had made together. They were to work out the details of Travis's collectible doll line and gather ideas on setting up his booth at the trade shows. He shared briefly about how he wanted a live runway show of models who would represent each of his dolls, and asked Jill to be his top model. Then, when the runway show would end, a few of the models would be in the booth to autograph purchased dolls they represented. They had agreed to spend the summer together to decide if they wanted to take the next step in their relationship, an engagement. But in an impulsive decision, Jill chose a career opportunity over Travis.

Her heart was now full of guilt for accepting a job the night of her graduation party. After her boss called during the party, she made the big announcement—a job position she couldn't refuse. Travis was in shock when he heard the surprise announcement. Later that evening, he read the letter Jill had handed him before announcing her decision. It was a letter she wrote explaining an anticipated career opportunity she hoped to get.

After her surprise news, Jill tried to smooth the situation over with him, but his heart was closed off. It was done. She had chosen her career over love.

***

Tara was asleep with a peaceful smile on her face. The night had ended better than if she had planned it herself. It was the final production of "Seven Brides for Seven Brothers," starring Brad as Benjamin and herself as Dorcas, his girlfriend. Tara had had a crush on Brad ever since seeing him a few years back in the musical, "Grease." He had the lead role of Danny Zuko, and when he wore the black leather jacket with his hair slicked back, it filled her with excitement. During their senior year of college, they had landed the lead parts of Curly and Annie in the musical "Oklahoma," which led them to performing in Seven Brides.

During the final cast curtain call, Brad surprised Tara with a bouquet of red roses. When she threw her arms around his neck with a squeeze of appreciation, he whispered in her ear, "Did you see Jill in the audience?"

Tara was caught off guard, not only for the roses, but also the question about Jill. She knew that Brad and Jill grew up as childhood friends. Tara fluffed it off as his being curious to see if his hometown buddy made it to their last performance. They discovered that Jill did not make it during their meet-and-greet with the audience. Tara was perfectly okay with that, as she did not like to share the attention of Brad with anyone. On the other hand, Brad seemed a bit disturbed that Jill was a no-show, and acted as if he were done with their friendship. He grabbed Tara's arm and told her they were going to the after-party together. Tara's heart pounded with excitement with the way he took charge of her, like a girlfriend.

The party was full of loud music, drinks and lots of dancing. Most of the music and dance moves were from the musical. Brad started out with a group of 'brothers' from the musical who gathered around the punchbowl.

One of the girls said that someone had spiked the punch. Tara made the comment to her, "Who needs liquor? I feel wonderful without it!"

The girl glared at Tara and walked away. Brad was the life of the party. He was in full swing on the dance floor, and when he spotted Tara, he pulled her onto the floor with him, swinging her around and around. Tara laughed as she felt her hair flowing through the air, enjoying the moment. Then Brad drew her in closer, and she could smell his cologne mixed with his sweat, a smell that only a girl in love would take in as an intimate fragrance.

When the music changed to a slow song of "I'm Gonna Love You Forever" by Randy Travis, Brad gently kissed her on the lips, then held her close while he sang the song in a whisper in her ear.

The night couldn't get much better for Tara. She was sold on the fact that Brad was in love with her, and she was his girl. He was in an incredibly good mood—a much different mood from when he had learned a few hours ago that Jill hadn't shown up for their last performance.

***

After Brad dropped Tara off at her house, he drove in silence for a while, his thoughts drifting back to Jill. The radio stations on his car didn't come in very clear on the back country roads, so he pushed a CD into his car stereo to the song, "In Case You Didn't Know."

He drove aimlessly, lost in his own thoughts, mostly about how disappointed he was with Jill. He decided that night while on the dance floor with Tara that he was done pining over Jill. He had been hopelessly in love with her since middle school. He took Tara in his arms on the dance floor, as if he were holding onto Jill. As the song played out about kissing the girl and how crazy he felt about her, he remembered back when he kissed Tara while dancing. He felt he was kissing Jill. His head was in a weird place, as if it were intertwining his feelings with his actions and the song lyrics that night.

Brad shook his head to try to make sense of it all. The passionate kiss that was meant for Jill had left Tara thinking she was his girl. He realized this when he dropped her off at her house and she told him she was so happy to have him as her boyfriend.

Brad felt sick to his stomach and a little dizzy as the words to the song hit home. He had never let Jill know about his true feelings for her, that he was crazy about her. Nor had he let Tara know that his heart wasn't into her, although tonight his actions played out as if he were.

He started to hum to the song and listened to the words like someone was in the car beside him. Brad felt his emotions change from a dreamy state of mind to frustration. He hit the gas pedal as he reached to change the track to another song. He put his focus back on the road and noticed fog was rolling across it. His mind couldn't stay focused. He tried to sing along to the next song but his thoughts were still on Jill and how she let him down by not coming to the last performance.

Brad reached over to the passenger seat where he had laid his cell phone and picked it up to text Jill. The bright light on his phone screen just about blinded him when he turned it on.

Focusing back at the road he noticed his visibility was getting dimmer as the heavy fog rolled in. Brad was determined to let Jill know how he felt about her, and how hurt he was about her not coming tonight. He tried to focus back on his phone screen to pull up Jill's name. With a glance at the road and back at his phone, his eyes opened wide to focus on what he wanted to type.

He found Jill's name and started to type: Jill I'm done! You have hurt me .... Just then Brad was distracted by a faint whistle sound; he looked away from his phone and back onto the road. He squinted, thinking he'd seen something ahead of him. But his ears were in tune to the words of the song playing on the CD. Maybe it was a train whistle on the music.

As the last line sang out about a destination being in the middle of nowhere, Brad wondered where he was. In the middle of nowhere? Where was he going? Why did he feel so disconnected from himself?

Brad opened his eyes wide as he continued to look ahead. Seeing something big in the middle of the road, he swerved back-and-forth as he slammed on the brakes, causing the car tires to squeal. The car fishtailed and skidded across the two-lane road. The car's momentum caused it to flip head over end into a small ravine. Brad heard a few words to the song as he felt he was floating in the air.

"Cling to the Father—don't ride that train. Watch out, Devil's drivin' that train." SSS CCC RRR EEE CH! Everything went black.

Chapter 2

It had been an emotional day for Sarah. One year ago today, her life began spiraling out of control. Her pain was so deep that it caused her to drift through the past year with a numbness in her soul.

She was thankful for meeting Jill in New York during a snow storm last fall, which led her to Gunner's Bed & Breakfast as a guest while attending Jill's graduation celebration.

After tucking her daughters, Tessa, Elise, and Aubrey into bed, Sarah quietly slipped out of their room at the B&B. She needed some fresh air. This was becoming a routine for her since that night.

The day she took her wedding vows, she'd never have guessed it would last only eight years. She married her first love, and thought that it would last forever. Now, she was on her own to raise their three young girls.

Sarah tip-toed cautiously down the spiral staircase to avoid the steps that squeaked as Travis's grandparents, Joe and Clara Gunner, were asleep on the first floor.

The crisp night is what she needed as sadness had closed in on her. The cool breeze brushed across her whole being while she looked up at the dark sky. Taking in a deep breath, she gently closed her eyes and lifted her arms out as wide as they would stretch, as if wanting someone to pick her up and hold her. She blew out her breath in an effort to release her pain. Warm tears streamed down her cheeks as she longed someday to be freed from her broken heart.

Walking toward the horse pasture she rested her foot on the lower fence board while leaning her arms and then her chin on the top rail. Listening to the different sounds of the night, while the horses munched on the grass, brought back so many memories of when it was just the two of them, Sarah and Cole.

She recalled, yelling, *No Cole! You're not going to win this race! I'll not be defeated!* The sound of hooves pounding the ground, and rhythmic puffs of air coming from the horses' nostrils was a moment in her life that was taken for granted, a time when life was carefree.

A few of the pasture horses moseyed toward her with a soft neigh. Sarah reached out her hand to pet the first greeter. Tears welled up in her eyes as the horse moved in closer and laid his muzzle on her shoulder. Cheek to cheek they stood as more tears released. She lifted her hand and rubbed the horse's jaw and audibly sobbed. "Why? I don't understand why!" Then the horse pressed in harder, as if he were holding her. Sarah reached up and hugged the horse's neck revealing her wounded heart to his hold.

Chapter 3

Tara rushed to the nurses' station and asked to speak to nurse Kate. The nurse looked up from the computer screen when she heard her name and immediately sensed who she was. Kate grabbed the patient's chart and stood to confer with Tara.

Tara felt sick and hugged her stomach as they approached the room. Monitors were beeping and the room was cold. Kate pulled the curtain back for Tara to identify the patient.

She gasped, "Oh, no—it's not Travis—it's—Brad!"

Tara's body started to tremble as she stared at Brad with all kinds of monitors and wires hooked up to him. Suddenly Tara felt warm and light-headed. Her knees buckled beneath her. Within seconds Kate saw Tara go limp to the ground.

Kate immediately called for help and went straight to her. "Tara, Tara can you hear me?"

Another nurse arrived as Tara began to mumble. Kate told Tara that she fainted and wanted for her to open her eyes. Once she opened her eyes, she tried to sit up, but Kate advised her to lie calmly while she took her pulse. The other nurse left the room to get Tara something to drink. Tears slowly rolled out of her eyes while lying on the floor. Kate offered her a tissue and reassurance that things would be okay. She and her friend were in the best hospital, and as soon as they were able to contact Brad's family doctor, the better they could assist him. Tara shook her head in agreement as she told Kate all the information she knew about Brad.

***

Tara was on the phone with Jill while looking out Brad's door at the nurses' station when his parents walked up.

"Oh Jill, Brad's parents just arrived. Call me when you know what time your plane gets in, and I'll pick you up from the airport."

Tara walked out of Brad's room, and put her hand gently on Carol's arm. Carol looked at her with fear in her eyes. "Where's Brad? Is he going to be okay?"

Tara tried to speak with a strong voice, "He's stable, but still unconscious."

The three of them walked over to his room. Tara hung back by the door as Brad's Mom and Dad walked up to his bed.

Tara whispered, "I think I'll be going now. Jill's plane will be flying in later this evening."

They both acknowledged with a nod of their head as she quietly walked away.

***

Jill was sitting on the plane with mixed emotions. All she wanted was to be in Travis' arms while he assured her that everything would be alright, like they used to be. She felt deep down inside that Brad's accident was her fault. It was the same emotion that lay heavy over her spirit when she saw the look in Travis's eyes when he heard her announce her decision of not spending the summer with him.

What is this career turning me into? Why is it so important to me to be successful in what I do? Look what it's doing to all my relationships. At least the ones that matter most to me, my boyfriend and my longtime friend.

The flight attendant's voice came over the speaker talking about landing. She blew out a long breath as she wasn't sure what condition she would see Brad in.

Jill spotted Tara as she walked off the plane. Waving her hands above her head she yelled, "Tara! Over here!"

Tara looked up, and shuffled through the crowd toward her. "I am so glad you're finally here. Jill, he looks awful! His face is swollen, and black and blue! He has all kinds of tubes hooked up to him…"

Jill grabbed Tara's arm and pulled her in close to her.

"Tara! okay, okay! I'm anxious to hear all the details, but let's hold this conversation until we get away from the crowd and in the car. Then you can tell me everything you know."

Tara nodded in agreement, saying, "Okay let's hurry. I want to get back to the hospital."

***

Jill ran toward Brad's parents once the elevator doors opened and she saw them walking toward her.

"Oh, I'm so sorry to hear about Brad! Can I see him?"

Carol sniffed as she wiped the tears that were welling up from her eyes. She shook her head, then buried her face into her husband's chest. Her husband wrapped his arms around her and cradled her closely as he reasoned the answer to Jill's question.

"Not right now…. He's still bleeding internally so he's being prepped for surgery. They need to find the bleeding and stop it."

Tara and Jill started crying as they backed away from Brad's parents. Tara dropped to the ground, and buried her head between her knees.

She mumbled, "What if I never get to see him again?"

Jill wrapped her arms around her stomach as it ached with tension. She looked up to the ceiling and pleaded in a desperate whisper.

"Oh Lord, please be with Brad and his doctors. Give them wisdom right now, Lord. Please stop the bleeding. In Jesus' name. Amen."

She bent down and put her arms around Tara and tried to reassure her that Brad would be okay.

***

Jill's phone buzzed silently in her hand while sitting in the waiting room with Brad's family, her parents, and Tara. In a state of despair and fatigue Jill glanced down at her phone. She sat up straighter when she saw the name on the screen. It was Travis. He was returning her call that she had left him earlier. She stood and excused herself from the room and she answered her phone.

"Hello."

"Hey, I just got your message. How's Brad doing?"

Jill closed her eyes and felt her body muscles relax a little, from the sound of Travis's voice. She took in a deep breath as if she was breathing in hope, and assurance that everything would be okay now.

"Hmm…well, I haven't seen him yet."

"What! Why? What's going on?"

"Well...Brad arrived at the hospital unconscious as they worked to keep him stable. When I got here, he was on his way to surgery. His blood pressure keeps dropping, so they need to find where he's bleeding internally. We've been sitting in the waiting room for several hours and haven't heard anything."

Travis was really concerned. "I am so sorry to hear this. I know how close you are to Brad. I will be praying for him. Jill remember, he's in God's care. Will you let me know when you hear from the doctors?"

All she wanted was to be physically close to Travis, to feel his arms around her. Tears rolled down her cheeks as she tried to gain control of her emotions.

"Yes, I will. I'll call you as soon as I hear something. Thanks for calling. It's good to hear your voice."

Travis cleared his throat before responding, "Yeah, thanks. It's good to hear your voice too. Well, I better let you go."

As they ended the call, he felt a tightness in his chest. Their breakup was so abrupt that they never got a chance to process it.

Jill walked back into the waiting room as Dr. Shadwick was shaking Brad's father's hand. She thought, it must be good news if they shook hands. Brad must be out of surgery and is going to recover.

Carol caught a glimpse of Jill out of the corner of her eye. "Brad's surgeon just gave us good news! He was able to stop the bleeding! Brad had a ruptured spleen which caused all the bleeding. He also had a testicular rupture which caused blood to leak into the scrotum. Thankfully, he is now in recovery and we should be able to see him shortly."

Jill let out a sigh of relief. "Thank you Jesus!"

She leaned toward Tara and as they hugged, she thanked her for all her help. Jill then excused herself to a corner of the room where she texted Travis with the good news.

The next morning Brad's family woke up in his hospital room to moaning sounds. He was becoming conscious and aware of his physical pain.

Excited to speak to Brad, Carol leaned over the bed rail with tears streaming from her eyes. "Brad, sweetheart, it's mom. Can you open your eyes?"

Brad had a tube in his nose down to his stomach to prevent aspiration. He winced at first but with a lift of his brows, his eyes flickered opened. Carol gasped with more tears streaming down her cheeks as she pressed the nurse's button. Brad was conscious.

Chapter 4

Travis was painting the front porch at the B&B when he got the call from Jill about Brad. She had shared with him about the spleen and testicular rupture and surgery, his broken pelvis requiring a brace and a dislocated shoulder. Jill further said Brad would need physical therapy once he was out of his brace and arm sling. Travis expressed his concerns and ended the conversation quickly when he saw Sarah and the girls walking toward the horse arena.

With a wave of his paint brush Travis yelled, "Hey...hey!"

Sarah looked over at Travis and held her hand out, motioning the girls to stop. They turned around and waved at Travis.

"Hi Travis, we're heading to the horse barn to watch the drill team practice their routine." Sarah's oldest daughter, Tessa, blurted out.

Sarah immediately spoke up, "Do you need some help painting the porch?"

Travis smiled as he responded quickly. "Only if you're offering." Then he chuckled.

Sarah motioned the girls to run along to the barn and walked toward the porch.

His faced lit up when he saw that she was serious about helping. He hated painting.

"So you're serious! I didn't think you would, seeing you were headed to the horse barn. I thought your kids said something to the fact that you were the best barrel racer and their daddy was the best bull rider."

Sarah's stomach gripped her as she turned her back toward Travis. She quickly grabbed a paintbrush and tried to respond in a nonchalant way. "Oh, you know how kids talk...they exaggerate sometimes." Wanting to get off the topic, she reached for the open paint can. "Where do you want me to start?"

Travis smiled. "Would you like to paint the spindles and hand-rails?"

"Sure." She offered a half smile as she drifted off in her own thoughts.

Travis broke the awkward silence between them. "So, Sarah, what's your story?"

She briefly stopped painting before replying, "What's my story? What do you want to know?"

"Well, you can start with what you feel comfortable sharing. I thought if I knew more about you, I could help you reach the goals of where you want to be this year."

Her mind went on alert. My goals. Where do I want to be this year? Why would he be asking me this? Maybe I'm not wanted here. What am I going to say? I have nowhere to go!

Travis put his hand on her shoulder. "Sarah…"

Tears were in her eyes as she looked at him. "Um, I'm sorry, I guess I haven't thought that far into the future." As she wiped away the falling tears she rambled on. "Have we overstayed our welcome? I mean, I am willing to work off our stay. I know that the bed & breakfast isn't up and running yet, but I'm willing to work wherever until it opens."

Travis didn't know what to say when he realized how the question made her feel.

"No, no, you and the girls are welcome here. I didn't mean to make you feel unwelcome." He rubbed her arm in a consoling way, "I would like to know you better so I can help you achieve what you want out of life."

She took in a deep breath. Her mind had been overwhelmed with thoughts about her life without Cole this past year. Being on her own raising their three young girls, she'd had no emotional energy left to put thoughts into her future. She collected herself, putting on a brave front before responding.

"I'm sorry for the tears. I don't want sympathy. I'm willing to work for our keep."

"Okay, let's start over. What did you used to do for a career?" Travis gave her some space and went back to painting the porch floor.

She dipped her brush into the paint and cleared her throat. "Well, before I had the girls I worked for a rodeo company traveling around."

Travis smiled, "Aw, so, that's how you became the champion barrel racer."

She smiled back at him. For a brief moment she felt good to think back to the beginning of where she started her career.

"You've been listening to my girls bragging."

"Well, yeah, I guess you could say they are pretty proud of you."

Sarah paused from painting as she continued to think back. "Well, okay, I'll admit riding a horse comes natural to me. So, entering barrel racing competitions was an easy way to make extra money."

They both continued painting as Clara walked up. "Hello, kids. I see the porch is getting a makeover."

Travis put down his paint roller and met his Grandma on the sidewalk with a hug. "Yes, it is. What are you up to today?"

She fumbled with a basket full of seed packets and some hand tools. "I'm heading to the garden."

Sarah perked up and eagerly offered to help her.

Clara glanced around trying to see how much painting was left to do. "Well, how much longer will you be painting, Dear?"

Shrugging her shoulders, she looked at Travis. "I don't know…How long will it take to finish?"

Travis smiled. "Um, maybe less than an hour." He glanced at his Grandma. "I think I'd better get back to painting so you can have my helper when we're done."

Grandma laughed. "Don't worry, Dear. I'm in no hurry. I'll go see what's going on at the barn. I'll meet up with you there."

Sarah felt a lift in her spirit. There was something about Clara that made her feel like she mattered. It was as though Clara could feel her loneliness and knew how to draw her in to her peace.

"Okay, I'll hurry…." she said, then she looked over toward Travis and added, "Without any mistakes, of course."

He nodded in agreement. "Don't worry, I'll be checking your work."

Sarah grinned and was suddenly in a better mood after talking to his grandma. As they continued painting, he could hear her humming softly to a familiar old country song. He wondered if she was thinking back to when her life was simpler.

Chapter 5

Jill was anxious to talk to Brad before flying back to Chicago. It was Tuesday before she had a chance to talk with him since his surgery on Sunday. She felt his family needed that time together, knowing he had tried to text her the night of the car crash, she wasn't too sure how he felt about seeing her.

That morning at breakfast, Tara told her she got accepted for a paid position on Broadway in New York. "Oh, my heart is torn! I don't know what to do. I know Brad will need my support during his recovery with being in the brace and sling. Ugh, why does it have to be at the same time that I should be in New York rehearsing?"

Jill nodded. "Yeah, wow. Bad timing huh? How is he taking it?"

"He's not really saying much. He's depressed, and withdrawn right now. When I'm with him I really don't know what to say. He hasn't said anything about the night of the accident. Well, at least not to me."

Jill's eyes widened. "Have you talked to his parents about it? Do they know what happened?"

Tara sighed, "All I heard was the police were coming today to take his statement."

Jill pushed her chair back from the table and stood by the window, wondering what happened that night. The nurse said there was a text on his phone to me, but I didn't get a text from him.

Tara scuffed her chair across the floor as she got up from the table. "What do you think caused the accident?"

Jill was relieved that Tara didn't seem to know about the supposed text to her, and she wasn't about to share that information with her now. "I don't know Tara, maybe we'll hear what Brad remembers."

"Are you going to see him today?"

Jill hesitated. "Well—do you think he wants to see me?"

Tara scrunched her eyes. "Why would you think he wouldn't want to see you?"

Jill dismissed the question by shaking her head. "I don't know. Did he mention me yesterday when you were with him?"

"Um, no, but I'm sure he would want to see you."

Jill stood quietly. She wasn't too sure about that. I wonder if he was texting me while he was driving, or if he remembers anything about the accident. The only way to get any answers is to talk with him, she decided.

Tara looked puzzled. "Jill?"

Jill quickly looked at Tara. "What? I'm sorry, I was thinking about all that Brad has gone through and wondering why or even how his accident happened."

Tara's voice was somber. "He's lucky to be alive."

Jill, still not comfortable with seeing him, asked, "Hey, would you go with me to the hospital?"

Tara nodded. "Sure, but let's not talk about my acceptance to Broadway just yet, okay?"

"Okay."

***

The Sheriff and a deputy walked out of Brad's room as Jill and Tara approached the nurses' station.

Jill stopped and pulled on Tara's arm. "Tara, what do you think Brad told them about the accident? Do you think he said anything about me?"

Tara shrugged her shoulders. "I don't know. Why are you acting so weird?"

Jill let go of Tara's arm and whispered. "Weird? What do you mean?"

Tara paused and looked at her. "You're acting like you played a part in the accident."

Jill swallowed hard before she responded. "What makes you say that?"

"Look—I know you can get a little in your head about everything being connected to you, but you weren't even with him that night. I was."

Jill's eyes grew wide. "What? I think everything is connected to me?"

Tara could feel her neck starting to blotch red. "I didn't mean it in a bad way. Well, I guess you could take it that way. I meant, you've been acting a little weird since the accident, like it was somehow your fault. Oh, come on, let's just go see Brad."

Brad's nurse was charting his vitals on the computer when the girls approached the room. Jill knocked on the door frame and waited for the nurse to look up. With a welcoming smile, the nurse motioned for them to come into the room.

"He's almost asleep. I think talking to the police officers wore him out. Lunch will be here soon, so maybe one of you can assist him with his meal."

Jill and Tara nodded in agreement and walked closer to Brad's bed. His eyes were closed so they decided to sit quietly until his lunch arrived. Jill's eyes welled with tears as she stared at Brad in his brace and arm sling.

"Dear Lord, if any of this is my fault, please help me to understand why, and how I can be a better person. I mean, if what Tara said is true, me being, 'all about myself' then help me to change so no one else gets hurt because of me."

Brad winced as he tried to reposition his right arm.

Jill immediately jumped to assist him. "Brad? It's Jill, are you awake?"

Brad's forehead wrinkled as he opened his eyes. "Jill? What are you doing here?"

"I came as soon as I heard about the accident. Do you want me to help you with anything?"

He closed his eyes for a few seconds, then he looked around the room and saw Tara. "Hey Tara. You're back."

Tara felt butterflies in her stomach and walked over to where Brad could see her better. "Yes, I'm back. Would you like me to do anything for you?"

He took in a deep breath and exhaled hard. "Yeah, can you raise the head of my bed up a little, about the same as yesterday."

Tara glanced at Jill nervously and started raising the bed position.

Jill felt the snub that Brad just gave her and wasn't comfortable with it. "Brad, I'm really sorry you're in here like this. I flew in from Chicago the night of your accident."

The room went silent as the bed stopped in the position he wanted. Tara's eyes roamed from Brad to Jill. She wasn't too sure what was going on between them.

A hospital staff rolled in a cart with Brad's lunch on it. "Good afternoon ladies. Will you be assisting our patient with his lunch today?"

Jill jumped at the offer. "Yes, I'll help him."

Tara backed away from the bed as she looked at Brad, "I think I'll run down to the cafeteria and get something to eat."

Brad acknowledged her with a nod of his head.

Jill took the lids off the bowls on the lunch tray. "You have cream of broccoli soup with crackers along with some applesauce."

She placed a straw in the bowl and lifted it to Brad's lips. His facial expressions showed he was hurting—not just physically but emotionally too—as he turned his head away from her.

Jill sat the bowl down and gently laid her hand on his forearm. "Brad, I'm so sorry if I did anything to hurt you. What happened that night? Do you remember?"

Brad closed his eyes and tears escaped from them. "I don't want to talk about it. It's over— and so is my life."

Jill was not expecting this, nor was she prepared to be an encourager. He was always there for her growing up.

Back when they were in elementary school, Jill fell off the playground slide and broke her arm during recess. For the rest of that year, Brad walked to school with her every day carrying her books and lunch bag.

"Oh don't say that! Your life is not over! You're here now. The doctors fixed you up and you'll be as good as new once you get your brace and sling off. Now here, you have to eat something." She lifted the straw to his lips again, but he turned away. "Come on Brad. Take a sip. It's the only way you're going to get your strength back."

Brad shook his head. "I'm not hungry."

"I know, but you have to eat. Would you rather have some applesauce?"

He pressed his lips tighter.

Jill didn't know what to say or do. She sat the bowl down and pushed the tray away from his bed. She had always had Brad to lean on, and now the roles were reversed.

Remembering back when they were in junior high, she had designed and sewn a three-piece outfit. Before the fashion competition she washed the outfit, and by putting it in the dryer, it shrank. Jill was devastated. She was to wear her design to be judged. Brad came up with the idea of displaying the outfit on her dressmaker dummy. He taught her how to turn tragedy into triumph—she won the competition. Now, in order to help Brad, she needed to know exactly what caused the accident.

"Brad? What happened the night of your accident?"

Brad blurted out. "Like you really care?"

Jill's head jolted as she looked at him. "What!?"

"You heard me. Why did you tell me you were coming to the show and then not show up?"

Jill stared at nothing. "The show… you mean the musical? Uh—I don't know—uhh I guess because of work." She looked back at him. "So you're upset with me because I didn't come to the musical?"

Brad looked at her with sincere hurt in his eyes. "I thought our friendship was more than you being a no-show! You could have at least left me a message as to why you weren't going to be there. I've always been there for you. I even tried to text you that night."

Jill was trying to think back as to why she didn't go to the musical. "Brad, I'm sorry. I've been so busy traveling with this new job. I guess I didn't realize that I hadn't called you when I knew I couldn't go. I'm here now for you, so please try to eat something—for me, please?"

Brad stared away from her. She grabbed the bowl again and leaned closer to him and realized the last thing he'd just said, 'I tried to text you that night'.

"Wait! —Oh! Oh, Brad, you weren't texting me while you were driving that night were you? Is that what caused you to wreck?"

Brad closed his eyes.

"Oh, Brad. No! It's my fault that you're in the hospital! I'm so, so, sorry! I'll make it up to you, I promise! I'm going to help you through this. I, I, can't believe it! It truly is my fault! I should have called you before you performed that night to tell you that I wasn't coming!"

Not knowing what to do next, Jill went into recovery mode. Nervously she lifted the bowl of soup near his mouth. "Here, will you please sip some of this soup? I'm not going to leave you, not until you're fully recovered."

One of the kitchen staff came in the room. "How's our patient doing? Is he finished?"

Tara walked in and looked at Brad's tray. "Brad, you didn't eat anything, are you okay?"

Jill asked the staff if she could come back later for his tray and she agreed.

"Tara, I'm just not up to eating right now."

"I understand. But, in order to get out of the hospital you have to build up your strength. So please, just eat the soup."

Brad looked at the straw, then leaned forward enough to let Jill know to assist him with the soup. Jill released her breath, not realizing she had been holding it. Her heart felt convicted more than ever about being responsible for the accident. She reminded herself to call her boss and request time off to be with him until he was released from the hospital.

Brad finished his soup, then Jill excused herself to make the call. But first she asked to speak to his nurse at the nurse's station. She wanted to see how long they thought he would be in the hospital.

Back in the room, Brad asked Tara what she is going to do now that the musical was over.

Tara was hesitant to say anything. "Um, I don't know, the first thing I want to do is help you with your therapy."

"It's not your fault that I had the accident. You don't need to take care of me. Jill said she would help."

Tara's eyes fluttered with his abrupt response. "Oh, well—I didn't realize she would be around to help you."

Brad muttered softly. "Well, it's the least she can do."

Jill walked back into the room. "I talked with your nurse and she said you are scheduled for your first physical therapy tomorrow. Also, I have a call into my boss requesting two weeks off, so I can help you with your therapy when they release you."

Suddenly, Tara felt like the third wheel in the room. Before the accident, she was under the impression that she was Brad's girlfriend. Now that Jill was back, she was a nobody again.

To gain self-worth, Tara stood and said, "Oh, by the way, I did get an offer to be on Broadway. They want me to fly out next week to seal the deal."

Brad's eyes widened in surprise. "What!? Well, that's great! I'm proud of you!"

That was the first positive emotion Brad had expressed or felt since his surgery.

Tara smiled. "Thanks! I'm not sure if I'm going to take it, though…."

Brad interrupted, "Hey now, don't even think about not taking it because of me! I have Jill here now to help me with my therapy. I will be fine without you. You go be a super star! You deserve it."

She didn't know how to take all of what he said—a slap in the face, but yet a compliment. Tara's heart hurt by the way he could dismiss her like that. They had just spent several months together rehearsing and performing in musicals together. How could he let her go so easily? Wasn't she his girlfriend?

Chapter 6

Sarah's chest tightened as she walked closer to the horse barn. The smell of horse sweat and leather used to be a scent that brought her joy. Now it was a painful reminder of what she used to have with Cole.

Tessa came running toward her. "Mama, can I join the rodeo drill team?"

Sarah reached out to hug her. "What?"

"I want to join the Grande Drill Team! It looks really fun riding horses to music with all their cool moves!"

Sarah released her hug, but kept her arm resting over her shoulders as they walked closer to the outdoor arena.

"Yeah, it does look like fun!"

The drill team was finishing up their practice. Elise and Aubrey waved at the girls as they exited the arena, then ran over to Sarah and Tessa. In unison they yelled, "Mama!"

Sarah smiled. They looked so happy. "Yes, my babies." She squatted down to hug them. "I suppose you want to be on the drill team too?"

Tessa jumped in with her opinion. "Mom, they're too young. However, I could ride with them since I've been riding my whole life."

Elise said with pride. "I know how to ride, too."

Tessa quickly finished her opinion. "Elise, you're too young; you're only six." Then she glared at Aubrey. "And, you don't even think about it since you are only four."

Sarah stood and told them. "Look, right now we are not in the position to own one horse, let alone three. So, let's enjoy being around the team, watching and learning; then maybe someday you'll all be on a drill team."

The girls wanted to go in the barn and watch the team untack their horses and watch as they hosed them off. Sarah agreed, and reminded them to stay out of the way, and to always let the horses know where they were so they wouldn't get hurt.

Tessa gently pushed the two younger sisters in the direction of the barn and assured Sarah she would keep an eye on them.

Sarah smiled. "Thanks, baby girl." She was pretty mature for being only eight. "You girls come down to the garden when you're finished. I'll be helping Clara with the planting."

Sarah lingered. As she stared at the empty arena, a memory of Cole crept into her thoughts. Cole sitting in the saddle with a group of girls standing around him. Seeing how she didn't like other girls around him, she would raise the bar to catch his attention. Flying around the barrels on her horse, Black Thunder, she caught Cole's eye. He would stop talking, and sit back in his saddle with an impressive smile on his face. That was one problem they had in their marriage—Cole was handsome, and with his bull riding skills, he attracted all the single girls who wanted to be with him.

Kicking the dirt beneath her, she hung her head down, wishing she could catch his attention once again.

"Shake it off Sarah, it's done. You can't change the past."

Slowly she strolled toward the garden, thankful for a purpose to live in the now, and not in the past. It was too painful.

***

"Hey Clara, I went to the horse barn after painting to find you weren't there."

Clara looked apologetic as she stuttered with her response. "Oh dear, I did say that I'd be there. Well, I did go, and I saw your girls were watching the drill team, so I moseyed on down to the garden. I'm sorry, Dear."

With an understanding nod, Sarah smiled. "What's the plan for this garden and how can I help?"

Clara pulled a cloth handkerchief out of her apron and dabbed her forehead. She walked over to her garden stand and fumbled through some packets of seeds.

"Well for starters, I would like to plant some green beans."

She handed Sarah several packets of seeds. Then she unhooked a 3-foot pvc pipe that was attached to the table.

"Here..." She handed her the pipe that Joe altered. "Grandpa made me this—to save my back from bending over to plant the seeds. Look here."

She took an opened pack of seeds and dropped one seed into the top of the pipe. The seed fell to the ground from the pointed end of the pipe. She waved her hand in a motion for Sarah to follow her to the already cultivated rows that she wanted to put the seeds in. Then she showed her how far apart to drop each seed.

Sarah was impressed with what Joe had made for Clara. "Now that's clever!"

They worked quietly for an hour planting green beans, peas, squash, watermelon, cucumber, and zucchini seeds. Clara wiped her forehead again and decided it was time to take a break.

"Let's go sit under the apple tree." Joe had made a bench that wrapped around the closest tree to the garden so Clara could have a shaded resting place.

"Whew!" Sarah said. "That sounds good to me."

Clara grabbed her small cooler and led the way. Once they settled on the bench, Clara opened her cooler and pulled out some kombucha tea. "Here you go. This will quench your thirst."

She unscrewed the cap and got a whiff of it. "Whew! What is this?"

Clara chuckled. "It's my own brew of fermented tea. Go on—take a swig. It's good for you, and will quench your thirst."

Hesitantly Sarah took a drink. Her eyes opened wide and her lips puckered. "Whoa! How potent is this?"

Clara laughed. "Not enough to make you forget all your troubles."

Sarah had a big grin on her face as she lifted up her bottle to Clara's. "Cheers to our friendship."

The bottles clanged together. They knew they had a special bond between them. As they sat enjoying the breeze, Clara was the first to break the silence. "So whatcha thinking about?"

Sarah replied, "Mmm—how I really enjoy spending time with you, and staying at the B&B."

Clara patted her knee while accepting her compliment. "Well that's sweet of you to say. What are your plans for the future?"

Sarah put her hand on top of Clara's and turned toward her with sadness in her eyes. "I don't know. I can't get myself to think about it."

"You've been hurt real bad, haven't you?"

Looking down at their hands, she answered Clara in a monotone voice. "You could say that. Ever since Cole went out of my life, I can't seem to see a future for myself. I barely make it day by day."

Clara positioned herself to put her arm around Sarah and pulled her in closer. "Have you prayed about your situation?"

"No, not really. I mean I've cried out sometimes, wanting someone to answer me, as to why it had to happen to me—to us."

Clara asked her, "So, do you believe there is someone greater out there who has the answers?"

Sarah shrugged her shoulders. "I don't really know...."

There was a faint sound of giggles and laughter that caught their attention. The girls were rolling down the hill toward them.

Sarah spoke first. "Well, I guess that's my cue to get the girls some lunch."

She stood and thanked Clara for the tea and led them back to the B&B for lunch.

Chapter 7

Brad was reading the report that the sheriff left him, along with his citation when Jill walked into his room. It had a court date on it with charges for reckless op and driving under the influence of alcohol.

"Hey there, whatcha reading?"

Brad turned the papers down and laid it on his brace. "Oh, nothing that concerns you."

Jill's eyebrows raised as she sarcastically said, "Wow, you're in a good mood."

He quickly changed the subject. "So, where's Tara?"

"Oh, she dropped me off; she had some errands to run."

Brad lifted his head in acknowledgment. "Hmm, I see. So what's this all about with her and possibly a position on Broadway?"

Not wanting to bring up the musical to remind him of her being a no-show, she hesitantly said. "Well, I guess they liked her in "Seven Brides for Seven Brothers"."

Brad had a look of despair in his eyes, as if his life was going nowhere. Jill saw the sad expression as he slowly nodded his head, acknowledging the facts. "Hmm…."

"Now Brad, you'll be back to normal in no time. I'm here to see to it."

"Jill, I have no future. I blew it! All because of …." He glared at her then looked away.

Jill's lips parted. "Uh...because of—me? Right?! That's how you feel?"

He lay there avoiding eye contact with her. His emotions were not in a good place. He blamed Jill for the accident. If she had come to his last performance as they had talked about, he wouldn't have had the accident. He glanced down at his citation, confused that it stated he was under the influence of alcohol.

Jill's eyes filled with tears as she looked away.

The rattle of the nurse's cart rolling into the room broke the silence. "Good morning. Brad, I'm Jeannie, here to take your vitals."

As she looked at the computer screen, she also informed him that he was signed up for P.T. at 10:30.

Jill wiped away her tears before she questioned Jeannie, "Would I be allowed to go with him?"

"Hmm, I don't see why not. Are you his girlfriend?"

Jill glanced at Brad before responding, "Sorta. I mean we've been friends all our lives, and we've always been there for each other. Well, he's always been there for me. So now it's my turn to be here for him."

Nurse Jeannie smiled as she took his temperature. "Well that's really nice of you. Yes, it would be nice for him to have a cheerleader."

***

Brad struggled during therapy. He was very shaky and worked up a sweat while using a set of light weights.

Jill stood motionless as she watched him struggle. Still feeling that the accident was her fault, she began to pray. *Dear Lord, please help him through this. I don't know what to do for him. Please show me how to help.*

Once they returned to his room, Jill grabbed a washcloth and ran warm water over it. She squeezed the water out and gently rubbed it over his forehead and temples. Brad closed his eyes, inhaled, and slowly let his breath out. He was physically and emotionally exhausted. With his eyes still closed, Jill could see tears escaping from them. She turned down the lights, scooted her chair next to his bed and lowered the bed rail. She laid her head on his good shoulder with her arm stretched across him, stroking the side of his neck in a soothing way. They stayed like this until he fell asleep.

Tara returned to Brad's room and stood in the doorway staring in silence for a few seconds. Not sure what she was seeing, she thought he might have received some bad news.

She walked in a little further, softly clearing her throat to catch Jill's attention. Jill lifted her head, then looked at Brad. He was in a deep sleep. The pain medicine had kicked in. She lifted her finger toward Tara acknowledging her. Then she tip-toed over to his bed table and opened the drawer. She wanted to leave him a note telling him she'd be back later. The only paper she could find were the papers from the sheriff. Jill paused for a moment wondering if she should read them.

Tara was curious as to what Jill was doing. She walked over to see. The temptation was too much. The girls read the citation, and their eyes grew big, their bottom jaws dropped when they read that he was under the influence of alcohol the night of his accident. Trying to hold in her disbelief, Jill quickly laid the papers back the way they were, and grabbed a napkin to write on.

Brad, be back later—Jill.

Once they got in the car, it was like a burst of water spewing out of a water balloon. Jill was the first to speak. "What was that all about? Alcohol?"

Tara was flabbergasted! "I don't know!"

Astonished, Jill continued. "Well, weren't you with him all evening?"

Tara felt offended and responded definitively. "Yes! And we weren't drinking! You know we don't drink!"

Feeling confused—Jill asked, "Do you think he went to an after party after he dropped you off?"

Tara shook her head in disbelief. "I don't know. He didn't say anything about going to one."

Wanting to get some answers, Jill thought if he was under the influence then maybe she wasn't to blame for his accident. She needed to find a way to get the timeline of when he dropped Tara off, when he texted her, and the time of the accident.

"Tara, what time did he drop you off that night?"

Tara took a moment to think before answering. "Um, let's see, the party was over at 11:00, so maybe around 11:30."

"And—did he say anything about going to another party?"

"I already told you. No!"

"Hmm." Jill started tapping her thumb on her lap. She zoned out from her surroundings, trying to think how she could find out what time he tried to call her, and when the accident happened.

"I know…I need to talk to nurse Kate from the emergency room, maybe she can help me put the pieces together."

Chapter 8

Sarah felt peaceful as she made the girls their lunch. Bobby Sue had reassured her time and again to make herself at home in the B&B kitchen. The Gunners made her feel protected from the reality of life until today, when Travis and Clara asked her about her future. She felt so alone when she started to think about it. Up until a year ago, she always had Cole. They had been inseparable since they were eighteen. They traveled the rodeo circuit together, kickin' up dust. She would turn the barrels, and he would ride the bulls. They were good as professionals.

As she watched the girls eat their lunch, she noticed how they dragged their grilled cheese through the apple sauce. A smile lifted her cheeks in a memory of Cole showing them how to do it—the cowboy way. There were no spoons needed, and with traveling all the time, it made a quick down-the-hatch lunch. She wondered if they missed spending time with their daddy. They seldom mentioned him. He loved having them around until right before show time. His character would change, to get in the zone, as he called it, for the competition.

The bull riders were the main attraction at the rodeos, and they had plenty of groupies who would follow them to all their performances. The owner counted on the bull riders to stay friendly with the groupies as a way to help fill the stadiums.

There was a particular gal named Rosa who always wanted to have her picture taken with Cole. It was one thing to see Cole in pictures with those kind of girls, but she couldn't stand the idea of his arm around them during a photo pose. It seemed that Rosa was obsessed with Cole, and he was either too polite or too blind to notice.

Sarah started to let herself flash back to the last rodeo that she and Cole did together. Images flashed of Rosa, Cole, bulls, the barrels, clowns, and the loud crowds in the stadium with flashing bright red and white lights. Suddenly, she felt her mouth go dry, and her throat tighten, making it hard to swallow. She stood quickly with an urge to run from the images. She couldn't let herself go back to that horrific night—the night that changed their lives forever.

Tessa noticed how her mama was acting, she'd seen this many times before. "Mama? Are you okay?"

The sound of her daughter's voice brought her back to reality. "Yes, Baby, I'm okay."

Tessa stared at her for a moment then hesitantly asked, "Mama, were you thinking about Daddy again?"

Sarah hid her pain from the girls most of the time, but seeing the drill team today triggered her memories of their last rodeo together.

"Yeah, but I'm okay now. How about we see if Travis could give us a lift into town to buy some ice cream?"

The two younger girls were excited. Tessa gave her mama an encouraging smile as her eyes looked deep within her, as though she could feel her mama's sorrow.

Sarah's mouth was still dry, which made it hard to swallow. She reached over Aubrey's shoulder and grabbed her glass of water. "Let's not waste this."

She continued to lift the glass to her mouth as she gestured with her hand for the girls to take their plates to the sink. With her mouth now moistened, she took a deep breath and felt better.

***

The girls loved riding in Travis's jeep, especially with the top off. Sarah leaned her head back against the leather seat, letting the wind and the sun consume her. Travis glanced at her with a smile as he could see she was relaxed and enjoying the ride.

When they pulled up to the ice cream shop, he told the girls it was his treat, and they could get whatever they wanted. They were so ecstatic that they couldn't get out of the jeep fast enough.

Sarah leaned over toward Travis and whispered, "Thank you! I'll pay you back—someday.

Travis grinned as he confessed, "Oh you already have…."

She wrinkled her forehead with a confused look. "How?"

"Well, I kinda gave you the hardest paint job on the porch. You know the spindles? So buying the ice cream will take the guilt off me."

Smiling, she nodded in agreement.

"Yeah, you're right. You did give me the harder job."

The girls were having a hard time deciding whether to have Superman ice cream, cookie dough or sorbet in a chocolate coated or cake cone. Sarah and Travis went for a cookies and cream blizzard. They all sat at a picnic table near the playground. Once everyone was done with their treats, the kids went off to play on the swings.

Travis was the first to break the silence between himself and Sarah. "So, I talked with my mom today to see if she needed any help at the barn, you know, as a paid position thinking you might want to work with the horses."

Sarah didn't move. Her eyes started roaming back and forth. *What? I can't! It's too painful to be around the horses, what am I going to say…?*

Travis leaned forward to connect eyes with her. "Hey—Sarah?"

Sarah recovered quickly. "Uh, yeah, sure. What did your mom say?"

"She said she would love to show you the schedule for running the horse facility. And, if you're interested in running it when she travels with the drill team that would be great."

Nodding slowly, Sarah asked. "So how often would that be?"

Travis shrugged his shoulder as he answered. "I'm not sure. But hey, if you're interested you could talk with my mom when we get back."

"Okay, sure. Like you said earlier, I need to think about my future, and getting a job is a start. Do you know when the B&B will be up and running? I would really like to work there."

Travis shook his head. "Boy, I don't know for sure. There is so much that my mom wants to upgrade. And I really don't have the time to do it. My doll production requires a lot of my time, but I don't want to leave my parents with all the responsibilities of the renovations."

Sarah liked hearing how Travis cared for his parents.

"Is there anything I can do to help you? Like a personal assistant? Or work with you on construction?"

He perked up. "Really? Even though I gave you the hardest part of the painting job, you'd be willing to work with me?"

She laughed. "Well, I might be selective on what I'll be willing to do."

Travis replied, "Oh, I see how this works. Okay, so selective work comes with a selective pay."

Sarah stuck her hand out. "I can deal with that. So—deal?"

Travis grinned. "Deal." He shook her hand and held it as he pulled her up to her feet and he continued. "Well, we better gather the girls, because there's work to be done back on the ranch."

Chapter 9

Travis was sitting at his desk when a face-time popped up on his phone. He looked over to see Sabrina's face. "Hey! What are you up to?"

Sabrina looked radiant with her pearly smile and the Tennessee summer glow on her face.

"How's my champ this morning?"

Travis leaned back on his chair and he gazed at her face before responding. "Aw, yes, we were the champs in your dad's pool last year. The famous chicken fight competition."

Sabrina smiled proudly. "That's right. That's why I'm calling you. Daddy is having a pool party for some of the doll vendors this Saturday. I know that you technically haven't started yet, but I'm hoping I can convince you to fly down and join us for the weekend. You can even stay in the guest house again."

"Oh, really? Well, does Gary know that you're inviting me to stay?"

"Daddy will be okay with it. And, knowing how business-minded you are, I could introduce you to some very successful people in the industry. Plus, we can talk about your booth for the doll show that's in the fall. You'll be ready by then, correct?"

Travis sat forward in his chair with a concerned reply. "Boy, I sure hope so. I'm working on a few inspirational dolls right now. I was hoping to be further along, but my parents have had me working on our family's Bed and Breakfast that they're wanting to reopen. There are a lot of upgrades needed, and changes to get everything up to code."

Sabrina was intrigued. "Hey, maybe Daddy will let me have a few days off so I could fly back with you and give you a hand."

Travis chuckled. "Wait a minute. Did I commit to your dad's party?"

Sabrina, with her ice-pink shimmering lip gloss, moved in closer to her monitor, offering Travis a pleading smile as she squirmed to say, "Well, I was thinking positive and wanted to offer myself to you. That's if you'd want me—to help?"

Shaking his head, he pointed his finger at her. "You—you know how to pour on the charm. Um…okay, let me see what I can do, and I'll get back with you."

Her face lit up while she clapped her hands together. "Sounds good! I'll let Daddy know that you're coming, and that I'll be going back with you for—uh, um, uh, a little while. Talk to you soon." She blew Travis a kiss and then she signed off.

Travis ended the call shaking his head. "She did it to me again! She's talked me into going. Man, she makes my head spin."

***

One positive response from Travis was all it took for Sabrina to make all the travel arrangements for them. He would arrive in Tennessee at 4:00 Friday night, so she could have him all to herself. Then the corporate pool party would be on Saturday, leaving Sunday open for whatever she could talk him into doing. They would both fly back to Ohio on Sunday night leaving her return flight open.

***

While sitting on the plane waiting for it to taxi to the runway, Travis could feel the nervous excitement in him. He wasn't used to being around a forward girl like Sabrina. When she liked someone, she wasn't afraid to show it. She had made it perfectly clear to him last summer that she was attracted to him.

Travis walked through the terminal wearing his tan cowboy hat and Durango boots, carrying a duffle bag. He tipped his hat when he spotted Sabrina. She always made him feel alive whenever he was around her—like an electric surge going through him. Travis needed a burst of joy in his life right now. He had suppressed his feelings for Jill, and it had had an affect on his creativity toward his dolls. The first doll was a replica of Jill, and slowly he'd been creating new ones.

Sabrina could not contain herself any longer. There was something about a cowboy's image that drove her crazy. She ran toward him. "Hello my Cowboy! It's so good to see you again!" She leaped into his arms hugging him.

Travis held onto her longer than he expected, as the fragrance of her perfume was a perfect mix of sweet and flowering freshness. He released her, but kept one arm rested on her lower back.

"Oh, so now I'm your cowboy? Whatever happened to being your champ?"

She laughed as she tried to explain herself, "Well, you do live on a horse farm, right?"

He agreed with a nod of his head.

"And it's a new year, so you might have to win another round of chicken fight to keep your 'champ' title."

Travis immediately took his hand off her back, waving it back and forth abruptly saying. "Uh…no way! You just about drowned me the last time."

She grabbed his hand and pulled him through the crowd as she ignored his comment. "Come on, let's get out of here!"

***

Sabrina opened the door to the guest house and led the way in.

Travis was inquisitive and a bit concerned as to why they were in the guest house. "What are we doing here, and where's your dad?"

She twirled back toward him and gave him a light kiss on the lips.

"Oh, he's probably golfing with some clients." She reached for his hands and pulled him toward the bathroom. "You—my dear, can change; then meet me at the pool."

She pushed him through the bathroom doorway as she turned and walked away.

Travis stood there feeling dumbfounded. "Uh, so I guess we are going for a swim?"

Sabrina smiled, then blew him a kiss and walked out the door.

Before Travis met Sabrina at the pool, he grabbed his phone to see how Sarah was doing stripping wallpaper in one of the bedrooms at the B&B.

"Hello?"

"Hey, it's Travis. How's it going?"

"Hey, boss! It's going good! I'm three walls in and one to go."

Travis had a smile on his face as he continued. "Really? That's great. It must be coming off pretty easy?"

Sarah offered a guilty laugh before spilling the beans that she had some help. "Well, I kinda had a little help today. Jill stopped in on her way home. I think she was hoping you would be here. She brought some homemade chocolate chip cookies with her, too."

"Hmm, did you happen to mention where I am?"

"Not really. I said you were gone for the weekend, and she looked disappointed. She said she needed to talk to you about something. I told her I'd have you call her when you get back."

Travis twitched his lips. The last time he was with Sabrina, Jill had reluctantly agreed to take a break with their relationship with one exception, that he would consider taking her to her school dance. She was going to college in Canton and he was in Columbus. They hardly spent any time together. Jill called him last year while he was at Sabrina's pool party. There was so much music and laughter going on that he couldn't hear her on the phone. She was not happy about it, and it wouldn't bring back any good memories if she knew he was with Sabrina again for the weekend.

"Okay, I'll call her when I get a chance. Hey, while I have you on the phone can you make sure that one of the single bedrooms is clean and ready for a guest?"

Without hesitation Sarah responded. "Sure boss, anything else?"

She couldn't see him grinning as he answered. "No, that's it. Thanks Sarah. I'll see you soon."

He walked over to the window as he put his phone away and spotted Sabrina on a pink flamingo floating around in the pool.

"Whoa! I better get a move on, or she'll be in here dragging me out to ride on that thing."

***

"Hey cowboy, what took you so long?"

Travis sat on the edge of the pool near Sabrina as she was slipping off her floaty.

"I had to make a phone call."

Making her way over to him, she reached out to pull him in. "All business and no play makes a man boring."

Travis eased himself into the water and gently used the palms of his hands to push her inviting hands backwards, creating space between them. "Well that's debatable."

Sabrina's brows lifted as she inquisitively asked, "So you say...how is it debatable?"

"Well you know how exciting a new project is, getting it up and running?"

She splashed her hands causing water to splash up on her. "Well—sorta—yeah."

Trying to get his playful side to come out, she reached for him, but this time she wasn't going to let him push her away. "Come on."

Wondering if he was shy or involved with Jill again, she just went for the question. "So, tell me—has anyone staked their claim on you?" She placed her hands on his shoulders.

Travis held her at the waist, an arm's length away. He looked into her blue eyes, not sure where he wanted this conversation to go. "Hmm, let's just say I'm selectively single right now. I'm devoting my time between the doll production and remodeling the B&B."

Sabrina pulled him in closer. "Well let's forget about all that today and enjoy each other's company."

She held onto him and suddenly pushed herself up from his shoulders and tried to dunk him. Travis flipped out from under her and grabbed her knees to flip her in a somersault. They continued playing like this until her Nanny came by the pool side.

"Sabrina, would you like me to bring you and your guest something light to eat?"

Sabrina had her arms around Travis's neck. She asked him with a nod of her head and he nodded back as he held onto her. "Yes, that sounds good. Thank you Sondra."

After Sondra left, Travis twirled her around and held her even tighter than before. "Hmm, how do you bring out the kid in me? I feel so relaxed right now."

She kissed his cheek several times. "Mmm, you're so cute when you're playful."

He chuckled. "And when I'm not?"

She pushed her lips out. "Then you're handsome."

On impulse he leaned in and softly kissed her lips, then gazed at her eyes as she came back for more.

Sondra walked toward the pool, explaining what was on the tray she was carrying. "I brought you kids some grapes, cheese and crackers, with freshly squeezed lemonade. Please let me know if you'd like anything else."

Sabrina smiled. "Oh that sounds good. Thank you, Sondra."

Travis released his embrace from her and grabbed her hand and led them both to the ladder. They settled in on the lounge chairs with the tray of snacks between them. Sabrina grabbed a small bunch of grapes and plucked one off and tossed it at Travis.

"Hey, wait! What are you doing?"

Giggling, Sabrina gestured for him to catch the next one with his mouth. He caught the third toss and grabbed the ones he missed with his hands.

"Okay, missy, lets see if you have any talent with this."

Nodding confidently, she smiled. "Bring it on!" She didn't miss a one.

Travis couldn't help but smile at her. "You're one of a kind."

"Yep! And I hope you like—my kind."

Travis winked at her. "Well—only the ones named Sabrina."

They laughed and then started to munch on the cheese and crackers. With full sun and a light breeze, it was a perfect setting to relax and sun bathe.

Sabrina asked Travis if he wanted some sunscreen rubbed on his back.

"You know, that's probably a good idea."

He reclined his lounge chair flat and adjusted the pillow so he could still see her.

She walked over and sat beside him. As she squeezed the lotion into her hands, she asked, "Hey Cowboy, I was thinking—maybe we could hang out here tonight, just the two of us, before all the craziness starts tomorrow?"

Travis was really mellow as she rubbed the sunscreen on his back. "Wow, that feels really good. I didn't realize how sore my back muscles were until you started rubbing them. So, uh, yeah we can do whatever you want. I'm up to taking it easy tonight."

She smiled then leaned down and kissed his cheek. "Thanks, Cowboy."

***

That evening they got into the hot tub after Sondra grilled steaks and potatoes and added a fresh garden salad.

Travis was enjoying himself and wanted to acknowledge Sabrina for it. "You know you're spoiling me?"

Sabrina took his arm and pulled it around her shoulders and said, "Yep, it's how a cowboy should be treated." She leaned her back up against him as she held onto his hand.

"But I'm not a real cowboy, ya know?"

"You are—in my eyes."

He pulled her into him and kissed the top of her head. "Oh, Sabrina, what am I going to do with you?"

She completely turned in toward him, causing the water to make waves. "Well, for starters, you could kiss me again."

He stared into her blue eyes, then looked down at her plush lips. With the lighting around the hot tub and the evening breeze, it was hard to resist her. Travis had never had a girl as affectionate with him as Sabrina was. They spent the evening in each other's arms watching a movie until they fell asleep on the deck.

Travis awoke to the pool guy whistling as he was getting ready to sweep the pool. He looked down to see Sabrina cuddled up beside him. He slowly pulled his arm out from around her neck, causing her to wake. "Um—I guess we fell asleep out here."

She stretched her arms out arching her torso while lifting her head. "Oh wow! Um, okay, I see Raphael is here to clean the pool. Do you want to come to the main house for breakfast?"

Travis felt uncomfortable after spending the night with her in his arms. "Uh, no thanks. I think I'll go take a shower and catch up with you later."

Sabrina tilted her head with pouty lips. "Are you okay—with last night?"

"Uh, yeah sure. I'll see you later—at the party." Travis picked up his towel and headed for the guest house

.

Book club questions for discussion.   *Chapters 1-9*

❖ *What's your perspective on Brad's accident? Was reckless driving the cause of his accident while listening to song lyrics, and letting them feed his emotions? Or was it from texting and driving? Or something else?*

❖ *Have you ever intertwined song lyrics with your emotions, allowing them to feed your emotions? If yes, did this empower you in a positive direction or a negative one?*

❖ *Have you experienced "a fragrance of love" like Tara described in Chapter 1? "She could smell his cologne mixed with his sweat, a smell that only a girl in love would take in as an intimate fragrance."*

❖ *Would you say Tara's description of a girlfriend to a guy in love is more like an infatuation or true love? "He grabbed Tara's arm and told her they were going to the after party together. Tara's heart pounded with excitement with the way he took charge of her, like a girlfriend."*

❖ *Do you think Brad was leading Tara on when he kissed her on the dance floor or was that a start of a potential relationship?*

❖ *Have you ever spiraled out of control—letting go of your surroundings and putting yourself in a position that led to a bad outcome? If yes, how did you recover? Were there certain scriptures that gave you the courage or strength to rectify any harmful actions or shame?*

Book club questions for discussion.   Chapters 1-9

❖ *What do you think changed Brad's actions toward Tara that night on the dance floor?*

❖ *Philippians 4:6 (NIV) "Do not be anxious about anything, but in every situation, by prayer and petition, with thanksgiving, present your requests to God." In Chapter 2, Sarah, a single mom of three, tried to hide her broken heart from others. She was drawn toward nature for comfort. How do you handle anxiety or a feeling of brokenness?*

❖ *Some pets have a way of comforting us with their gentle presence. Can you think of a time when an animal comforted you when no one else could?*

❖ *Have you ever felt sadness as deep as Sarah expressed in Chapter 2, with wanting someone to hold her?*

❖ *In Chapter 3, Jill expressed that once she would talk to Travis it would be like breathing in hope and assurance that everything would be okay with Brad. Who is the person who can give you hope when talking to them during rough times?*

Book club questions for discussion.   Chapters 1-9

❖ *When tragedy happens to those we love we tend to reflect back to see if there was something we could have done differently to prevent it. Do you think Jill could have prevented Brad's accident?*

❖ *When Travis asked Sarah about her future goals in Chapter 4, he could sense she needed encouragement. What are some ways you could push yourself or others through rough times, to have hope in the future?*

❖ *When Tara was sitting in Brad's hospital room with Jill, she felt like a "third wheel." Have you ever been caught in a crossfire, jeopardizing your emotions?*

❖ *Should Jill blame herself for Brad's actions—texting and driving? Why or why not?*

❖ *In Chapter 5, Brad's bitterness hurt Tara's feelings and blamed Jill for the accident. Do you think he should take some responsibility for his own actions?*

❖ *Have you been in a relationship where you were more invested than the other person? Did the relationship last?*

Book club questions for discussion.   Chapters 1-9

- ❖ *Jill showed spiritual maturity when she prayed for her eyes to be opened toward her flaws. Have you prayed a similar prayer? If yes, did you receive a positive outcome?*

- ❖ *Whoa! In Chapter 7, Brad was charged with driving under the influence of alcohol. Now what do you suppose caused the accident?*

- ❖ *In Chapter 8, Sarah expressed her concerns about Rosa. Do you think jealousy played a part in her anxiety?*

- ❖ *Emotions are powerful! They can control our daily decisions if we allow them to. That's why the Bible says to renew our mind with the word of God. Read the following Bible verses. Proverbs 3:5, 6, Psalm51:10, Ephesians 4:23 and Romans 12:2*

Chapter 10

Jill had a spring in her step when she walked into Brad's hospital room carrying coffee and donuts. "Good morning Brad. I brought you some of your favs."

Brad eyed the box that she was carrying. "Mmm…cream filled?"

She giggled as she sat the box on his table. "Yes! One with chocolate icing and the other with caramel."

"Let me guess who gets the chocolate one? Hmm.…"

She opened the lid and handed him a donut. "Ha-ha, I wonder who?" She was happy to see him joking around. "I got you a vanilla mocha latte to go with your caramel cream filled donut. I thought we both need a little kick to start packing you up to go home."

Brad took the donut from Jill as she started packing. "Yes, thank you! I need something to perk me up. I can't wait to get out of here. What time will my mom be here?"

"She's here now. We rode together. She's with Home Health trying to finalize your therapy orders. We decided to ride together so one of us could ride in the transportation van with you, and the other will drive the car."

He took a sip of his latte then nodded. "Okay, cool. So—how much time did you get off work?"

Jill quickly replied. "Well, they agreed that I could have the rest of this week off and then re-evaluate the situation. You know, see how therapy goes."

Brad's doctor walked in and eyed the donut box. "Hello. Mmm, I see you are enjoying the finest donuts in town."

Brad laid down his donut and reached out his hand to greet him. "Yes, Dr. Shadwick, my friend, Jill, knows how to perk a guy up, through his stomach."

Jill giggled. "Yep, works like a charm."

The doctor looked down at Brad's chart with a grin on his face. He then directed his attention toward Jill. "If you would excuse us, I have to go over some test results before signing his release forms."

Jill acknowledged with a nod and walked quickly out of the room.

Brad looked concerned. "Is everything okay?"

Dr. Shadwick sat down in the chair beside him and let out a long sigh.

"For the most part it seems to be. But—I have some bad news about your scrotal injury. You have permanent damage and it has potentially reduced your sperm count. I'm sorry, but due to the heaviness of the blow to your testicles and scrotum in the accident, you have a 95 - 100 % chance of being sterile.

Brad looked confused. "What actually are you saying...I—I can't have children?"

"It's very unlikely you will have any viable sperm. However, the good news is—you're able to be released today and start physical therapy. I don't see any reason why you won't make a full recovery."

Brad stared past the doctor, repeating to himself what the doctor just told him. *95-100% chance of being sterile.*

Dr. Shadwick stood and laid the papers in front of him. If you could sign these. I will have my nurse contact you for a follow-up in a few weeks. Do you have any questions?"

With the lift of his brows he shook his head and signed the paper. Dr. Shadwick handed him a copy. They shook hands and he left quietly. Moments later, Jill and Brad's mom, Carol, entered his room.

"We are all set to go. I saw Dr. Shadwick in the hallway and he said that you're a lucky man to come out of an accident like yours with minimal injuries. Are you ready?"

Brad looked at his mom. "Ready as I can be."

He pushed aside his donut and handed the papers to Jill. "Could you pack these away?"

"Sure, no problem. Oh, your mom and I talked, and we decided that I should ride in the transportation van with you and she will stop on the way home to get your pain medicine filled."

Brad lifted his head with a nod in response as his mom was folding his bed cover. The transportation team arrived and was positioning Brad to be escorted to the van.

Jill picked up on his subdued mood and wondered what the doctor had told him. With the test results in her hand, she turned her back to Brad and glanced over them before putting them in his bag. After scanning them quickly, she saw nothing to account for a mood change. Then she saw Dr. Shadwick's notes. Sterile. What? Brad's sterile—so does that mean he can't have children?" Jill was so flustered that she tripped over the leg of the chair as she moved to put the papers in his bag.

"Oh, sorry guys. I'm a little clumsy. I guess a double shot of espresso was not what the doctor ordered for me today!"

***

Brad was showing signs of pain during the ride home as the pain medicine hadn't kicked in yet.

Jill's mind was racing in different directions. *So, if he is sterile, is this a sign that he is the one that I'm supposed to be with? Is this why the accident happened? With me not wanting children and he can't have any? Maybe it's my fault. But what about the alcohol they said was in his system? Am I where I'm supposed to be—with Brad?*

She looked over at him. He was resting with his eyes closed. The pain medicine finally kicked in. She ran her fingers through his hair and rested her cheek on his forehead.

'Dear Lord, if this is who I'm supposed to be with, then please let me feel the passion for him that I felt for Travis. Amen.'

Chapter11

Sarah frantically hustled around the B&B as she barked orders to her girls. "Tessa, Elise, go get the sheets out of the dryer. Aubrey, you can help mama by dusting." She kept looking at her watch. "Uh, where did the time go? Travis will be here soon with his guest!"

Aubrey looked at her. "It's okay, Travis is a nice guy. He won't be mad at us if the room's not ready. Smile, Mommy."

She paused and smiled. "You're right, baby girl, he is a nice guy. I wanted to surprise him with the decorations that we just hung, and I'd lost track of time."

Her other daughters walked into the room with a hand full of bedding. "Here you go, Mom."

"Oh, thanks." She grabbed the warm sheets and started to make the bed. "Okay girls, run down to the kitchen and see if Clara has the tray ready. If she does, carefully bring it up and put it on the table by the balcony."

The girls hustled out of the room proudly, they loved the idea of helping the adults run the B&B. Clara and the girls made banana bread, and Sarah thought it would be nice to put one in the guest room for Sabrina. She also made sure the room's refrigerator was stocked with bottled water.

***

Time flew by for Travis and Sabrina on their flight home as they talked about the trade show. Jonah caught up with them while they were standing in line for her luggage.

"Hey, man. I'm glad you finally made it. I was wondering if that car of yours kicked the bucket."

Jonah grinned. "No, it's still going. There was an accident that caused the delay." Looking at Sabrina, he continued, "So are you going to introduce me to this pretty lady?"

Sabrina offered her hand. "Hi. I'm Sabrina Curry. You must be Travis's business partner and long-time friend?"

Jonah shook her hand. "Yes, I see you were well informed. We grew up together. So, I hear you are in the toy trade show industry?"

"Yes, well, my father, Gary Curry is the one who is the founder of our business. But I guess you could say I'm the CEO." She giggled, then pointed to her black and beige leopard luggage. "Oh, Travis, can you grab my luggage?" He reached for a very large suit case. "Oh, and that one, too."

Jonah looked surprised by the amount of luggage she had. "So how long are you planning to stay?"

She pulled the tow handle up on her suitcase and smirked. "Oh, one never knows."

Travis and Jonah smiled as they grabbed the rest of her luggage.

Sabrina had to sit on Travis's lap as her luggage filled the whole back seat.

Jonah glanced over at Travis. "Uh, I'm guessing I should have brought your truck?"

Sabrina glanced at Travis. "I'm not too heavy for you, am I, Cowboy?"

Jonah arched one eyebrow as he looked at Travis. "Cowboy?"

Travis rolled his eyes. "Uh, yeah, I guess if your name is Sabrina and live in Tennessee, wearing a cowboy hat makes you automatically a cowboy."

She flipped her arm around his neck and kissed his cheek. "And a darn cute one at that."

Travis felt very uncomfortable, so he changed the topic. "So Jonah, why don't you tell Sabrina about our thoughts of adding a book with each of our dolls?"

Jonah picked up on Travis's awkwardness, so he began telling her how the books would be written in a way to encourage and uplift kids to think better of themselves and their situation—to be the best they can be.

***

Bobby Sue, Clara, Greta, and Sarah were sitting on the porch swings watching the girls' gymnastics moves when they pulled up to the B&B. Greta was the first off the porch to greet them. She was surprised to see Sabrina climbing off Travis's lap.

"Whoa! You guys were packed in there!"

Sabrina offered her hand to Greta. "Hello, I'm Sabrina Curry."

Clara caught up with them and reached to hug Sabrina. "Clara Gunner. I'm Travis's grandmother—and a hugger. Welcome to our B&B."

"Thank you. I'm looking forward to staying here with Travis."

Clara's eyes widened just enough for Bobby Sue to read her reaction—that this gal is interested in Travis.

After they all introduced themselves, Jonah waved goodbye to Travis and took off.

Greta grabbed Travis's arm as she questioned him. "Um, so what are the plans?"

"Well, Sabrina has offered to help me with the renovations here."

Greta tilted her head to one side.

She threw a quick glance at Sabrina's suitcases then back at her brother. "Really? She must be planning on staying a while."

Sabrina was making over the girls' pigtails and admiring how curly Aubrey's were. Sarah told her that her own hair curls up in the humid air, too. They went on with the conversation about the Ohio weather while Greta gave her brother that sisterly look—you better keep your guard up with Sabrina.

Sabrina walked over to them. "Hey Cowboy, whatcha say you show me to my room so I can change for that horseback ride you promised me?"

Greta's eyes about popped out of her head. "Horseback ride—you promised her?"

Travis could feel his sister's vibes about Sabrina and the fact that he would offer her a horseback ride. She wasn't too keen on Sabrina. "Well, it's more like I owe it than it is a promise."

Nodding her head, Greta folded her arms and was enjoying Travis trying to explain himself.

"You see, it's just that she wanted me to play the game of 'chicken fight' at the pool party like I was persuaded into last year. So I told her that I would take her horseback riding instead."

Everyone laughed, and Travis grabbed her luggage and headed for the door. Clara informed her that she would be staying in the Delilah room that had a balcony overlooking the equestrian facility.

One of the girls exclaimed, "Oh, that means you're rooming beside us!" Great!"

Sabrina smiled.

Tessa was in awe of Sabrina. Her heavy eyeliner accented her big blue eyes. Her stylish haircut—short textured reddish blonde hair, with long bangs parted to one side, hung jaggedly over the opposite cheekbone. Her clothing was fashionably young—short jean skirt had a lightly fringed bottom. With it, she wore a yellow and powder blue paisley midriff shirt unbuttoned to reveal a matching blue camisole. Her ankle-high cowgirl boots completed the picture.

Trailing behind Sabrina and the girls, Greta whispered. "So, Travis, what horse is she going to ride? Rowdy?"

He gave her a stern look as he responded. "No! She's never ridden a horse before. I don't think a rodeo horse would be a good fit."

"Yeah, maybe not—but it would make a good show."

Travis hurried ahead to catch up with Sabrina while Greta stopped at the welcome counter with an ornery grin on her face.

Bobby Sue shook her head once she saw the look on Greta's face. "Greta, what are you up to?"

With her lips pressed together Greta smiled before saying, "Well, if she is dressed to impress, let's see if she can impress him around horses." She waved at her mom and headed out the door.

***

Travis and Sarah were standing in the hallway one door down from Sabrina's room looking at the newly painted walls. Travis was quite impressed. "Great job, Sarah!"

"Thanks, Boss, but…I can't take all the credit. Jill helped some, too. Oh, by the way, did you call her?"

"Oh shoot! I better do that now."

Sabrina's door was propped open by one of her luggage bags. She could hear Travis talking on the phone at the end of the hall. She thought she heard him say Jill's name. Stepping closer to the door she heard Jill's voice on his speakerphone talking about a designers' runway competition in New York. She was excited to go and hoped to gain some creative ideas for his doll fashions.

Sabrina immediately went into competition mode. Grabbing her phone, she searched for designers' runway competitions in New York. Bing! *There it is.* She scrolled down to see when and how to enter. *Perfect! It's in two weeks. I can stay here until then and fly to New York for the competition. I've got this! Travis will depend on me even more. I can't wait to tell Daddy; this will be good for our business too.* She filled out the entry form, and sent a text to her dad with the link attached to it.

Travis told Jill that he thought she would enjoy it, and hoped she would win the contest. Then he asked about Brad. "How's he settling in?"

"It was a rough ride home, but he's sitting out on the porch talking to the neighbors. They brought some pot luck food over, and his dad is grilling burgers."

"That's good to hear. So you're staying at your parents' house?"

"Yep, right across the street. I told him I'd go to P.T. with him."

Sabrina startled him with a hug around his waist when she snuck up on him.

"OHHHH! I mean, okay. Hey, listen, I have to run. It was good talking with you. Tell Brad I said hi, and I'm glad he's home."

Sabrina giggled as she squeezed him harder. "Teeheehee."

Jill was inquisitive about what she heard, "Travis? Are you okay?"

Travis tried to pull out of Sabrina's arms. "Uh yeah, let me know how your competition goes. Talk to you then. Bye"

Jill held the phone wondering what was going on with him. "Yeah sure—bye."

After ending the call, she dialed Tara's number to see if she could stay with her while in New York. "Hey Tara, it's me!"

"Jill! How's everything back home?"

"Oh, pretty good. Brad's home, and we'll start home therapy this week once we meet the therapist. How's New York?"

"Better than I expected. The days are long at rehearsals, but the cast members are really cool. I'm sorry that I haven't kept in touch—

with Brad and all. I just thought I would make a clean break from him and everything else."

"What do you mean—everything else?"

Tara didn't want to say why she left so abruptly but it was the only way she knew to protect her heart. Brad wasn't in love with her as she had thought. Brad was in love with Jill, and she had to accept it and move on.

"Oh his accident and stuff..."

Jill interrupted, "Oh, I did find out that he tried to text me right before the crash. Apparently he was mad at me for not calling or coming to the last performance. I feel really awful."

Tara didn't want to dredge up those old emotions. "Well, I'm glad you're there for him. I wish him the best."

"Yeah, I don't know if I'll ever be able to make it up to him, but I'm here, and it's a start. Oh, you'll never believe what came in the mail."

Tara blew out a sigh of relief for the change of subject. "What?"

"I'm going to a runway show competition!"

"What?!"

"Yep! And guess where it is going to be held?"

"No...New York?"

Jill giggled with joy. "Yep! So, I thought we could meet up while I'm there or maybe—I could stay with you?"

"Yes, that sounds great! When?"

Jill fumbled with the envelope to check the date on the letter. "Oh, here it is. It's in two weeks."

"Okay. That should work. Hey, did you ever find out anything about the alcohol that was on Brad's report?"

Jill sighed heavily. "Nope."

"Well, I remembered. While we were at the dance party, I heard a girl say the punch was spiked."

Jill's mouth dropped open. "What?! You just now remembered this?"

Tara went into her nervous, fast chattering. "Well, I don't know, I guess I didn't consider Brad drinking it. I mean—he could have. Maybe that's why he was so—so friendly with me on the dance floor. Oh! Why didn't I see the real picture before? Here I thought he was really in to me that night, and now I have to believe that it was because he drank the spiked punch. Oh Jill, I feel like such a fool!"

"Now, come on Tara. Pull yourself together. You don't know if he drank the punch. Let me talk with him, and see what he says about the punch."

Tara was nodding her head in agreement with Jill. "Okay. Let me know. Hey I've got to go."

"Okay, I'll see you soon."

Jill was anxious to talk with Brad. He had a court appearance this morning, and she wanted to know what he said about the alcohol level they found in him.

Chapter 12

Jill was excited to see Brad arrive home. She stepped off her front porch and ran across the street to greet his mom. "Hi Carol. How did it go?"

Carol gave Jill a hug. "Oh, I think for the most part it went well. He's still confused about the alcohol report. Someone must have slipped something in his drink the night of the after-party."

Brad's dad pushed his wheelchair around the van to the temporary ramp they made and got Brad up on the porch.

Jill couldn't wait for the chance to tell Brad what Tara had told her about the spiked punch.

"So, because of the DUI charges and the fact it was his first citation, he has to take an on-line alcohol awareness course, and they suspended his driver's license for three months. But, who knows when he'll be ready to drive again?"

She was glad he didn't get a harsh penalty. "I would say he was lucky."

Carol shook her head in agreement. "Would you like to stay for lunch?"

"Yeah, sure. I'll hang out with Brad until then."

Jill walked over to the porch and sat down beside him. "How ya feelin'?"

"Relieved that court is over. I feel…I feel so paralyzed. I'm stuck in this brace for who knows how long. I don't have a car or a job and I can't do anything for myself. I feel really helpless and I hate it! I hate it!"

"Okay, let's break this down." She was trying to respond without her emotions. "First of all, you're lucky to be alive…and that no one else was involved in the accident. Secondly, I know about the

DUI charges, and this was not a careless act of drinking and driving. Tara told me something today that I think you should know."

He looked over at her, surprised by what she just said. "What? Wait—how did you know about the DUI?"

Not wanting him to know she first found out by reading the citation report at the hospital, she led him to believe it was through their moms. "Well, first of all, our moms are best friends and you know...."

"Okay, yeah, yeah go on."

"Tara said she'd remembered a girl at the after-party had mentioned that the punch was spiked."

Brad leaned forward in his wheelchair and stared at her. "What!? Are you kidding me?"

Jill nodded her head. "That's what she said."

"Did she say anything else?"

Jill didn't know how much she should share, but she thought he had the right to know so he could apologize to Tara for his actions.

"Well, she now realizes that your actions toward her were not the way you really felt and that she wasn't your girlfriend after all. This was why she left abruptly for New York."

Jill jumped when he hit his fist on the arm of the wheelchair, catching her off guard.

"Grgh! I had no idea that the punch was spiked. Why didn't she say something to me? I mean, thinking back, I had an attitude about not caring about you, so I put my focus on her. I thought we had a great night dancing, but I didn't realize that I made her feel like she was my girl until I dropped her off."

He went silent as he continued to think back to where he could see the vision of him kissing Tara passionately on the dance floor. The kiss, in his mind, was a kiss for Jill. "Oh boy, I totally messed things up."

Carol brought lunch to them. "Now if you need anything else, just holler."

"Thanks, Carol."

"Thanks, Mom."

"You're welcome."

Jill organized Brad's lunch in front of him. "Brad, don't be so hard on yourself. You didn't know the punch was spiked, or the fact that Tara's feelings were more involved where you're concerned."

"Jill, stop! You're wrong! Okay, maybe you're right about one thing—I didn't know about the alcohol in the punch. But Tara, I felt she was more into me than I wanted, but that didn't mean that I didn't like her as a friend. And to be honest about the kiss on the dance floor…well…I…it…never mind. I think I need to talk to her about it. I owe her an apology; she's a great girl, and I feel really bad about how our friendship parted."

Jill felt the pressure of guilt rise in her throat. She wanted to talk to him about the text he tried to send her the night of the accident. She stood and paced back and forth.

"Brad, can I ask you something?"

He moved his head and chair around to where he could see her. "Yeah, sure. What?"

"Well, how much do you remember about the night of the accident?"

"I remember taking Tara to the dance, then taking her home."

"Okay…."

"Then—I remember driving in the dark, with a flash of a bright light and fog, then black again."

Jill stooped down to look at him eye level with her hands on the arms of his chair. "Go on."

He stared into her eyes wanting to be held by her. Then, he barely shook his head ever so slightly. "That's it—that's all I remember."

Jill was so anxious to hear more, that she didn't realize she was holding her breath. Exhaling as she let go of his chair, she stood and turned from him and wondered. *He doesn't remember texting me? Should I ask him?*

Brad waited, "Jill?"

"Huh?" She was confused about the text on his phone and not on hers.

"What's bothering you? Do you know something about that night that I don't?"

"You said that you remembered texting me that night—were you driving and texting?"

He looked off into the distance as his lips twitched. "I remember being upset with you, about your not calling or showing up at the production." His mind flashed, seeing a burst of bright light. "I don't remember when I texted you—I…"

Carol walked up and cleared her throat. "Would either of you like dessert? I have warm brownies and vanilla bean ice cream."

Frustrated with Brad's lack of memory, Jill sighed then put a smile on and looked at Carol. "Absolutely! That sounds great. I'll come help you dish the ice cream."

She knew she had to tell him that she learned he crashed the car by texting and driving. It all lined up, the time the text was written on his phone, and when he lost control of the vehicle, causing the text not to go through to her phone.

Chapter 13

Greta was turning the horses out to the pasture when she caught a glimpse of Travis and Sabrina walking toward the barn. She wasn't too fond of Sabrina's character, and the fact that Travis didn't know if she was a Christian or not. Her mannerisms and appearance gave Greta the impression she wasn't—or if she was, she didn't have a personal relationship with the Lord.

Greta wanted to see her brother happy, but was protective of him. She and her whole family were surprised by Jill's sudden change of heart when she decided to take a new career position this summer and left Travis abruptly.

"Hey guys! Whatcha up to—cashing in on a promise?"

Travis gave Greta the caution eye as his left eyebrow arched before answering. "Yep, I thought I would show her around the farm on horseback."

Greta smirked. "So Travis, who is she going to ride?"

He immediately replied, "Oscar!"

Sabrina looked at them with concern. "Is that a nice horse?"

Oscar was an old foundation quarter horse that Travis and Greta learned how to ride on. He was in his mid-twenties but still able to enjoy a trail ride.

Greta quickly reassured her. "Yes, he is. You don't have a thing to worry about. My brother will take good care of you."

Travis felt relieved that Greta reassured Sabrina, and he hoped she would go on her way and leave them alone. She had a way of reading girls and relationships. He didn't want to be analyzed or admit any differences in his relationship with Sabrina. And he surely didn't want to hear it from her. It was refreshing to have someone who wanted to be with him and put him first.

74

Sabrina looked relieved. "Well, okay then, I think I'm ready to ride Oscar."

Travis grabbed her hand and led her to the stalls. "See ya later."

Greta kicked the dirt beneath her as she lifted her head and nodded.

Sabrina was all giggles as they walked away. They both seemed to be enjoying each other's company, but Greta was concerned about her intentions, and her beliefs. Next to loving the Lord, she loved her brother.

***

Travis held Oscar's reins as he gave instruction to Sabrina. "Okay—put your left foot in the stirrup and hop up into the saddle while swinging your right foot across his back."

Sabrina let out a nervous giggle. "Okay." Her first attempt didn't go so well. When she hopped up she came right back down and got her foot caught in the stirrup.

"Travis! Help!"

He came around to the side of Oscar and pulled her foot out. Then, he put his hands around her hips. "Okay, put your foot in the stirrup again and on a count of three, I want you to push off with the foot on the ground. One—two—three." He lifted her up and onto the saddle.

"Whew! Okay, now that I'm up here what do you want me to do?"

Travis smiled as he handed her the reins. "Well, for starters, grab these reins and just sit tight as I grab a horse for me."

"Whoa, you're just going to leave me here?"

"You'll be fine. You're in an enclosed arena; what could go wrong? I'm going to grab a few things and saddle up my horse."

As he walked away, Sabrina looked around to see no one in sight. She let go of the reins, and pulled her phone out from her back pocket, and clicked the camera icon. The view was beautiful, with rolling hills in crops of hay, outlined with trees, and wild ducks swimming in the pond. Adjusting her phone to take a selfie with the view as her back drop, she started to pose and clicked away. Oscar blew out of his nostrils and he shook his head. It startled Sabrina, and she dropped her phone.

"Oh! No! Travis?" Oscar felt her body tense up and started to prance around. "Oh! Oh! Stop, horse!" She grabbed hold of the saddle horn and squeezed her legs tightly for fear she would fall off. Oscar was confused by her signals and started to trot forward. Sabrina was now screaming, "Travis! Help!"

Travis came running out of the barn as Oscar picked up speed, causing Sabrina to lose her balance.

He ran to the opposite side of the arena to slow Oscar down holding his arms out in front of him. "Whoa—Oscar! Whoa!"

Once Oscar turned the corner of the arena and was heading toward Travis, he came right to him and stopped. Sabrina was hunched forward over the saddle horn.

"Oh! Travis, I want down. Get me off this horse. Now!"

He looked up at her, trying to stay composed. With one hand on her thigh and the other hand holding the reins, he asked, "What happened?"

With a huff she sat up and straightened her shirt. "Well, for starters I was taking pictures with my phone, and all of a sudden this horse…" as she points to Oscar, "decides to take off, causing me to drop my phone. I tried to hang on for dear life, and that's when he kept going faster and faster. Can you please get me off this horse? I don't want to ride after all."

With a humorous smirk Travis timidly asked, "Did you happen to tighten your legs around him?"

"Well—yeah…how else was I going to stay on?"

"That's how you cue a horse to move forward, keeping your legs squeezed tells him to move faster. Come on, let's get you off the horse, and go find your phone."

Sabrina was without words as she dismounted from the horse and hugged tightly to Travis.

Travis rubbed her back in a consoling way as he held her close. "I'm so sorry that happened. I guess I'm not used to someone not knowing how to ride a horse. Listen, I'm going to keep my promise…."

Sabrina pulled back from him. "Oh, no. Um, that's okay—the deal's off."

Putting his arm around her as they walked Oscar back to the barn, he came up with a new plan to keep his promise to her. "How about we ride double?"

"Double? You mean we both ride the same horse?"

"Yep. I'll take the reins, and you ride behind the saddle."

She was quiet for a moment before responding, "Mm, well, maybe that would be okay—I guess."

"Good! Hey, I think I see your phone."

Looking toward the direction he pointed to, she ran ahead, picked it up and clicked it on. "Oh whew! It works!" She tapped the camera icon and took a picture of Travis and Oscar.

Chapter 14

Carol grabbed the ice cream from the freezer and handed it to Jill. "I wanted to tell you that I just got off the phone with Travis's mom. She and I were thinking Brad could help them with the renovations of the B&B."

Jill eyes widened brightly. "Really? But—how?"

"Well, he did graduate with a construction engineering degree. So—Bobby Sue thought it would be great if he oversees the upgrades to the B&B. That would free Travis to work on his doll line and give Brad a purpose while he's confined to a wheelchair. What do you think?"

"That sounds great!" She plopped a scoop of ice cream on the plate. She thought, *Maybe I could drive Brad over there now and have a chance to run into Travis.*

"Carol, do you think I could drive your van and take Brad there today?"

"Oh! Well, I suppose that would be alright. Let me get in touch with Bobby Sue and see if that would work with her schedule."

Jill was hopeful that Travis would be there.

***

As they pulled up to the B&B parking area, Jill noticed Travis's jeep. It was parked in the adjoining parking lot facing the equestrian center. Excitement fluttered in her stomach.

Maybe Travis is close by and would help me get Brad out of the van. Then, while Brad is in a meeting with his parents, we could take a walk and talk. I'm almost done with this summer position and, who knows, maybe we could pick up where we left off.

***

Bobby Sue and Bo waved as she put the van in park. Jill smiled. She wasn't sure how they felt about her with the way she broke things off with their son.

They had offered the B&B to Brad and her to have their college graduation party. That's when and where she announced that she would be taking a new summer position. She left a letter with Travis explaining her sudden reasons why she wouldn't be spending the summer with him. They had hoped that living close to each other would lead them to an engagement. Now she is back in town due to Brad's situation, but still in an emotional turmoil as her heart mourns for Travis's affection. She carried guilty feelings over Brad's accident, thinking it could have been avoided if she'd contacted him before his performance.

Slipping out of the driver's seat she gave them a hug. "Hi, how are you guys?"

In unison, they said they were good.

Bo walked around the van to greet Brad, who was in the back seat. They shook hands and discussed the procedure of how to get him out of the van. Once he was settled in his wheelchair, Jill offered to sit on the porch swing while they went in and around the B&B to show him what their goals were for the renovation. She had high hopes of seeing Travis.

***

Sabrina was feeling more comfortable on the back of Oscar, now that she had her arms wrapped tightly around Travis's waist. The two of them were trotting closer to the pond where he'd planned a picnic.

"Whoa, buddy."

Travis pulled his foot out of one stirrup and told her to slide her leg down Oscar's side and put her foot into the stirrup, while swinging the other leg around to dismount. She was a little ill-at-ease, but managed to do it.

"Whew, I think I need a drink after today."

Travis untied a small duffle bag from the saddle along with a jean quilt. "Well, you'll have to settle for bottled water, because that's all this cowboy has to offer."

He tossed her the quilt. She unfolded the quilt laying it close to the waterline. "Is this okay?"

Unhooking the bit and reins from Oscar's halter-bridle, he looked over at her. "Yep. That looks like a good place for a picnic." Then, he patted Oscar and left him to graze.

In the duffle bag he pulled out two bottles of water and handed her one.

"Oh, thanks!"

He gave her a sandwich and placed the bag of grapes in the center of the blanket along with some cheese and crackers. They both plopped down on the blanket, ready to chow down on lunch.

***

Sarah was weeding the garden when she heard laughter coming from the pond. She walked toward the laughter. Up ahead she could see Travis and Sabrina sitting by the edge of the pond

Oh, that's right, he was going to show her around on horseback. But, I only see one horse. She asked herself. *Ya suppose they rode double?*

Her mind drifted back to a time when she and Cole used to ride double before they had the girls. Tears welled up in her eyes. *Sarah, stop it! You're never going to get over him if you keep living in the past.*

She decided it was time to quit for the day and head back to the B&B.

***

Travis and Sabrina had finished their lunch when they somehow got into a tickling match. Rolling around on the quilt, he finally pinned her down and made her promise to stop tickling him.

With her arms pinned above her head, each catching their breath, he impulsively went in for a kiss. Suddenly, the mood changed, making it a more romantic setting.

He released her arms and cupped her face gently, not wanting to stop kissing her. She embraced him. Then he slowly rolled her over and they lay in each other's arms.

Sabrina was the only girl that made Travis feel the desire to be intimate with her. Deep down he knew it wasn't right to feel this way when they didn't have a committed relationship. They had actually only known each other a little over a year, and a long distance relationship had not helped. So he didn't understand his feelings. Intimacy was one thing missing in his relationship with Jill.

Sabrina grabbed her phone that was vibrating in her back pocket. "Oh, hey, sorry it's my Dad. I have to take this."

Travis sat up and nodded. "Sure, no problem."

He got up and walked over to Oscar, who was grazing on some alfalfa grass. Sitting down beside him he looked out over the pond. The last time he was at this pond was when he had read the good-bye letter from Jill the night of her graduation party. She had handed him a letter before she stepped on the stage to announce that she'd decided to take a job position for the summer. He was deeply hurt by her actions.

After that, he began to put up walls around his heart. Today, thinking back over that whole ordeal, he thought to himself. *Hmm, after what I just felt with Sabrina, I don't think I was hurt emotionally by Jill's actions as much as I felt betrayed.*

Sabrina sat down beside him. "You okay?"

"Uh-yeah. Coming to this pond cleared up some things I've been wrestling with. So yeah, I'm good."

They smiled at each other and let the quietness linger before packing up and heading back to the stables.

***

Jill walked around to the side porch, hoping to see Travis as she gazed over the hay fields. She stopped and studied two people riding on a horse. Staring at them, she realized it was Travis and a girl with short strawberry blonde hair. It puzzled her, as she couldn't think of any of their friends fitting that description.

Talking to herself, she questioned her theory, *Uhh…I wonder who that is and why they are riding together? Maybe one of the boarders was thrown from her horse, and Travis went to give her a ride back to the barn.*

Brad was writing notes on a printout that Bobby Sue gave him with all the upgrades. Maneuvering around in his wheelchair outside the back porch he saw Jill standing at the corner of the house.

"Hey, Jill, whatcha looking at?"

She was so intently focused on seeing who Travis was with that she was startled by Brad's voice. Quickly turning her gaze toward him, she saw Sarah making her way toward the porch. Sarah had gathered some wild flowers to give to Clara, who stayed with the girls to see where they lagged in their education. They had fallen behind with always being on the move. In order to get them caught up, Clara suggested homeschooling them while they lived at the B&B.

"Oh, hey, Sarah." Jill said as she waved to her.

Brad shook his head. "'Oh, hey Sarah'? What are you talking about?"

Jill walked up to him, grinning. "Sorry. Sarah is behind you."

Brad pivoted his chair around to see Sarah cresting the top of the hill. Something inside him woke up. His heart pumped an extra beat seeing her blonde hair flowing off her shoulders carrying wild flowers.

Brad whispered. "Whoa—Sarah—that's the Sarah with the three little girls?"

Brad was taken by her natural beauty. As she got closer he could see the sadness in her eyes, the same sadness she had at their graduation party.

"Oh, hey Jill. What brings you here?"

Jill greeted her with a hug, then re-introduced Brad to her. "Do you remember Brad? We had our graduation party here?"

Her face creased with her smile, and she reached out her hand. "Oh, yeah. Hi. I'm sorry to hear about your accident."

Brad shook her hand. "Yeah, it could have been worse." Directing his attention to Jill, he continued, "Hey, I'm just finishing up here, then I'm free to do whatever."

Jill blinked a few times as she looked at him. "Free to do whatever—um okay." She was surprised he actually was up to doing something. Maybe bringing him to the ranch with a purpose is what the doctor ordered. "What are you doing right now?"

"Oh, writing up a material list to close in this back porch. They want it done first thing before the weather gets cold."

Sarah had a surprised look on her face. "Oh, so are you going to help with the renovations?"

He nodded his head, and grinned. "Yeah—yeah, I think so."

Jill smiled, then put her focus back on the two riding horseback as they were getting closer. She could definitely see that it was Travis.

"Sarah, that's Travis, right? And who's on the horse with him?"

Sarah looked to where Travis and Sabrina were riding together, and her voiced dropped to a lower tone. "Yep—and it's complicated and not worth talking about."

Brad looked at both girls watching him and wondered if they both had a thing for Travis.

Sarah broke her stare—away from them. "Well, I better get these flowers in a vase." Looking down at Brad she continued, "Hopefully I'll see you around."

"Yeah, I would like that." Brad watched her walk into the B&B as he turned toward Jill. "Hey, are you about ready to go?"

"Um—yeah, I guess so." Jill's chest felt heavy, and her heart hurt. Walking behind Brad's chair, her thoughts were in a self-seeking place. *Everything is so wrong. I've messed up everything by taking the job offer the night of my grad party. Travis is no longer mine. Brad's accident is my fault, too. He wouldn't be in a wheelchair and not able to have children if it weren't for my being too busy to care about him instead of my commitments.*

Jill was quiet on the ride home.

"Hey, so what's Sarah's story?"

Jill glanced at Brad through the rearview mirror. "Well—we met in New York, ya know?"

"Yep—yep. But why is she at the B&B?"

"She had no place to go. The aunt she was living with in New York was placed in a nursing home, and her house was foreclosed. So when I made arrangements for them to come to our graduation party, Bobby Sue offered her a room at the B&B and work around the farm."

"Hmm. So she lives at the B&B?"

"For now."

"What's the story with the kids' dad?"

"I don't know. I haven't had time to talk to her."

Jill thought to herself. *Wow, I can't believe how self-absorbed I have been since I graduated. I don't know any more about Sarah and her story than when we first met in New York last December. I need to spend more time with her.*

Chapter 15

Jill's nerves were getting to her while sitting in the auditorium reading over the rules for the designer's competition.

Station one: Pick two to three fabrics to create a runway model

Station two: Pick 5 embellishments

Station three: Design your runway model within 90 minutes.

Once everyone had made their model and placed it on the judging table, they sat in the auditorium. Jill flipped through her phone while waiting on the results and was distracted by a high-pitched voice. Looking forward two rows ahead and two seats to her left she traced the voice. Staring at the girl, she thought her hair looked familiar. She then focused on what the girl was so chatty about and heard the name Travis.

Jill gasped quietly. *Oh no way! It couldn't be the girl I saw on the back of the horse with Travis the other day?* Leaning forward, she was now more than ever wanting to hear what she was talking about.

"Oh, I'm sorry, I forgot to introduce myself." She reached over to shake the girl's hand beside her. "I'm Sabrina, the CEO of my daddy's trade show company. I coordinate all the vendor's booths, and now I have a new vendor coming on board who wants a runway for live models to represent his collectable dolls. He'll be so proud of me if I win this competition…."

Jill's ears were burning. *It can't be! That's Sabrina! Here at this competition?*

"Good afternoon ladies. Just a few more minutes, and we will have the results for the winner. We would like to thank each and every one of you who came out and gave us your designer ideas. We will be implementing the winner's design at our next winter fashion show. And photos of the winner will appear in our magazine."

Jill felt sick to her stomach. *What is going on here? Why is she here? And what was she doing at the ranch the other day!?* She couldn't keep her eyes off of her. If eyes were lasers, she would have burned a hole right through Sabrina's head.

"Thank you for your patience. We would now like to announce our winner. All the way from Tennessee, Sabrina Curry! Would you come forward?"

Jill's shoulders rounded forward as her chin dropped to her chest. With all the applause and Sabrina's squeaky voice, she was done. She stood and excused herself from the seating area and headed for Tara's place.

***

Jill knocked on Tara's door. "Tara? It's me, are you home?"

Tara opened the door. "Hey, you're early. Come on in."

The girls embraced, then headed toward the couch.

"Wow, this is a cute apartment."

"Thanks, I like it. Hey, do you want something to drink?"

Jill plopped down on the couch. "Oh, I'll take whatever you have if it can fix my broken heart."

Tara handed her a glass of iced tea. "What? I thought you went to a competition. What's this talk about a broken heart?"

Jill took a sip of her tea then set it down on the end table. "I did, and you're not going to believe who was there."

Tara's eyes grew big with anticipation and wondered aloud. "You knew someone at the competition—here in New York?"

"Yep!" Jill responded with a big sigh. "Have a seat. This might take a while to fill you in."

Jill started from the beginning when Travis first went to Tennessee last year to meet with Sabrina's father about the doll trade show, and built a friendship with Sabrina, to seeing him with her this past weekend at the B&B riding double on a horse.

"So, you mean to tell me Travis stayed in contact with her and you saw this same girl at the competition today? So, what happened? Did you have a confrontation with her?"

Jill stood and walked to the sliding glass door that led to a small balcony before responding. Taking in a deep breath she looked at the view of New York City.

"Wow, I have made a mess of my life. And look at you—you've stayed true to yourself and pursued your goals. All I've done is ruin my life and everyone else's around me."

Tara shook her head and walked over to her. She turned, looking Jill straight in her eyes. "What happened today?"

Jill frowned. "Oh, it's not just today; it's everything leading up to today. And, well, Sabrina winning the competition today and hearing her talk about Travis made me think if I would have handled my desires to make it in the career world differently, I'd still have my relationship with him, and maybe Brad wouldn't have had his accident. And you, well I don't know…I guess it did work out for you."

"Okay. Let's take one thing at a time. Sabrina was at the competition and you know it was the same girl that Travis met in Tennessee because you heard her talking about him, right?"

Jill nodded.

"Did she know who you were?"

"No, we never really talked. She sat in front of me, and I recognized her hair cut from seeing her on the back of the horse with Travis. That's another long story. But, then I focused on her conversation and heard his name. Now seriously, how many guys named Travis are there in the doll-making business? Then, when they announced the winner from Tennessee! BAM! It confirmed it. It was Sabrina. Ohh—why was she there? How did we both end up at the same competition in New York?"

Tara didn't know the answer. She was a bit confused and baffled by the whole story.

"Um—wow, that's kinda crazy. I'm sorry, Jill."

She opened the sliding door and they both walked onto the balcony and leaned over the banister. After they stood in silence, Tara was the first to speak.

"Jill, it sounds like you're still in love with Travis."

With tears in her eyes, Jill nodded. "I am. But we still have different views about having children. And now with Brad not being able to have…"

Tara looked concerned. "Brad? What? What's going on with Brad?"

Jill cleared her throat. "Oh, nothing. I mean, with his life put on hold until he's healed from the car accident, he feels down in the dumps." She quickly turned from Tara and walked back into the condo thinking she almost spilled the beans about Brad being infertile.

Tara followed behind her. "Look. We can't change the past, so let's focus on the future. With that being said, you only have one day in New York, so let's go exploring."

Jill smiled. "Sounds good. Let's go shopping; it always makes me feel better."

Chapter 16

Brad was in good spirits when he arrived at the B&B. He had gotten his brace off. Wearing a new brace around his torso gave him the ability to move more freely.

Clara and Sarah greeted him and his mom in the driveway.

"Well, hello."

The ladies hugged each other. "Hi Clara, it's so nice of you and your family to let Brad bunk here while he assists the construction crew with the renovations."

"Oh dear, he will be a big asset to us. Come. Let's sit on the porch swing while Sarah helps Brad get settled in."

"Are you sure? I can…"

"Yes, I'm sure. She's helping out around here while Bobby Sue and Bo are out of town with the drill team."

Sarah smiled at Brad. "Yep, I'm at your service."

Brad's hand pushed his wheelchair over to the steps.

"Well, I see the first thing we need is to install a handicap ramp."

Sarah groaned. "Um, about that—the B&B is not handicapped accessible, so you will be staying in a room that is attached to the lounge at the stables."

"I'm sleeping in the horse barn?"

Sarah wrinkled her nose. "Um—just until you reconstruct a bathroom in one of the lower level rooms at the B&B. Bo said you could use it as your office. He even mounted a piece of plywood over the steps off the back porch as a ramp to get in and out with your wheelchair. Do you want me to push you back there?"

He shook his head. "No thanks. Now that I have this new brace I can manage this myself." He turned his wheelchair toward the side of the house that led to the back porch. "Oh could you toss my gym bag and pillow to me?"

She grabbed his bag and pillow out of the van. With the toss of the pillow he reached up to grab it, but she walked over to place the bag on his lap. "Do you have anything else?"

"Um… yeah, my laptop. It should be in the back seat."

Once she grabbed his laptop, she tucked it under her arm and followed him to the back porch.

Brad looked at the temporary ramp that Bo put on.

"Uh. O—kay, well you might have to give me a little push onto the ramp. I see that I'm going to have to modify this to be able to come and go without assistance."

Sarah looked at the depth span from the square edge of the board to the ground. She giggled. "He was in a hurry to put this on before they left. Here, you take the laptop and I'll give you a push."

Her hair fell over his shoulder brushing his cheek as she leaned over him to set the laptop on his lap. With the smell of her sweet perfume and the feel of her hair, Brad had a sudden mood lift.

Standing straight, she grabbed the chair handles and gave it a push. Then she maneuvered herself around his wheelchair and opened the door. Their eyes met. He noticed they were a little brighter than the last time he was there.

With a shy giggle she motioned with her hand. "Follow me. The room is down this hall, across from Clara and Joe's room."

Following her into the B&B he asked, "So—are you staying here at the B&B?"

"Yep. Me and my three girls. Our room is above yours, actually." She smiled at him as she stopped to open the door.

"Here you are. I've customized the room with a small refrigerator, along with an office desk for your laptop. And—oh yeah, I thought you might want some exercise stretch bands and free-weights too—you know, to rebuild your strength."

Brad was impressed with her thoughtfulness.

"Wow. You thought of everything I'd need to work and to keep improving my recovery. Thank you."

They smiled at each other as their eyes locked in again, but this time it was for a longer hold. Feelings of compassion flooded her as she blinked away her stare. She walked over to the bathroom door and flipped on the light.

"As you can see, the bathroom will need to be converted to be handicap friendly. Um, can you think of anything else you might need?"

Brad laid his laptop on the desk. He looked around, trying to focus on the question and not on her long, sandy-blonde hair and petite frame.

"No, I can't think of anything right now. I really appreciate your help. My situation is only temporary, so when I get out of this chair—someday, I want to do something nice for you."

Sarah stopped her body motion as she walked toward the window. She turned her face toward his and smiled. "Okay. I might have to hold you to that offer."

They held eye contact and—for a split second—she felt hope and was excited for that... *Someday*. She glanced out the window and asked if he was ready to see his living quarters.

He chuckled, as he wheeled his chair to the window. Pulling back the curtains, he eyed the horse barn. "You mean—that barn?"

"Uh—yep, that would be the one."

He laughed while tossing his hands up. "Okay, I'm up for the adventure."

"Great!"

Brad grinned. He had a good feeling about this job and about Sarah.

***

As her plane lifted in the air. Jill was sulking over the fact that Sabrina won the runway competition. She looked out the window, lost in her own thoughts. *She may have won the competition, but I'm going to see to it she doesn't win Travis's heart.* She heard a text come in on her phone. It was from Brad.

"Great news!" Brad typed. "At my doctor's visit they decided to take my first cast off and replaced it with a more mobile one to support my hips. I have so much more mobility now. I decided to move to the B&B and start my new job. I hope you can stop in on your way home to see my new brace. Love, B."

The text made her smile. She was really happy for Brad and told him she would definitely stop by. She tucked her phone away and felt a little emotional pressure lift. Brad was getting his independence and his life back. Where did that leave their relationship? Her emotions were bouncing around within her. Thinking she belonged with Brad when she found out he was infertile, because of her not wanting children, to having jealous feelings over Sabrina and Travis having some sort of a relationship. Could she really let go of Travis or rethink her decisions about having children? That was the only thing they couldn't agree on. Maybe she'd jumped into her career too soon. But she knew she would thrive on success.

Where do I belong, and with whom do I belong?

The plane jolted, causing her to be more aware of her surroundings. She sat up straighter and looked around to see that most of the people on the plane were businesslike people. There were no children. She grabbed her laptop and went to her search bar. *Now what!* She tapped her thumb on the keyboard. *Hmm—I know, I'll create a competition to put on Travis's web site. Let's see… Sabrina may be better at runways, but she can't beat me when it comes to fashion. We can have people pick out fabric designs that they want to see on a doll of their choice, and I will choose the winning fabric, and design the outfit. The winner will win a free admission to the doll trade show to see the fabric they chose on one of the live dolls.* She had a positive focus for the rest of the flight home as she typed out the details for the fashion competition.

Jill pulled in at the B&B on her way home from the airport as promised to Brad. She wasn't too sure who she'd run into. Would Sabrina be there? Travis? She didn't know if they were in a relationship now.

"Hey, come on in. The room is small with this wheelchair, but look—I got my brace off." Brad puffed up his chest as he slapped it with his hands.

Jill shut the door behind her. "That's great! How long will you be in the new brace?"

"I'm not sure, but the doctors were impressed with my progress. Now I can do more for myself. I can get in and out of bed. Watch." He flipped the foot rest up on his wheelchair and maneuvered his chair around the room with his feet!

"Whoa, that's great! It won't be long before you're up and walking. What's with this sudden move to the B&B? I go away for a long weekend, then I get a text from you saying you've moved in. And—in the barn?"

Brad smirked. "Yeah. After I got my brace off, I felt like moving forward with the job offer I got the other day. So with short notice, the barn room was the only one that would work with a wheelchair. The washer and dryer are in the bathroom. According to Sarah, they wash their horse blankets, saddle pads and leg wraps in there. My life has been on hold too long due to the accident. I would have agreed to sleep in a tent just to have a purpose to focus on."

With sincerity, Jill said. "Well, you can't keep a good man down…so, should I let my boss know that I'm able to go back to work?"

He glanced out the window and saw Sarah and her girls standing at the outdoor arena and smiled. "Hmm—yeah, I think so. I think I'll get along just fine here."

Jill looked out the window too. "Hey, Sarah and the girls are here. Let's go talk with them."

"Uh, yeah sure."

***

"Oh Travis! We must celebrate my big win when we see each other again."

He was caught by surprise with the story of how she won the runway competition that Jill went to.

"So—Sabrina, how did you hear about this competition?"

"Oh, let's leave the petty details alone. I want to know when I'll see you again?"

"Well, I'm not sure." Travis saw Brad and Jill talking to Sarah and the girls as he pulled up at the ranch. "Can I get back with you on that? I'm at the ranch, and I need to talk to Brad about the renovations."

Travis didn't pick up on Sabrina's disappointment as she questioned him. "You promise you'll call me back?"

"Um, yeah. Talk soon. Bye." He parked the jeep and hopped out as he put his phone away. Jill caught a glimpse of him heading their way and excused herself. She was anxious to talk to him alone about his relationship with Sabrina and her new idea for his doll line.

"Well, this is a surprise. What brings you here?"

Jill's smile was from ear to ear. "Well, Brad asked me to stop in on my way home from New York."

Travis felt obligated—but awkward—to ask the question that he knew the answer to. "Oh yeah—how did it go?"

Jill's smile dropped to pouting lips. "Mmm—let's say it didn't go how I thought it would."

She cleared her throat while wondering if she wanted to bring up Sabrina's name. But, she thought, it's now or never. "Did you mention anything to your friend Sabrina about the competition?"

"Uh, no why?"

"Well, Sabrina Curry, from Tennessee was the winner."

He studied her expression as he voiced. "Well, maybe they invited all the CEOs from the trade show industry."

"Yeah, maybe. Um, are you seeing her now?"

"Well, we keep in touch and all. You know, with me trying to get my dolls exposed in the marketing world."

Jill gave him a dead stare. "Travis?"

"What? You mean like a girlfriend?"

Tears welled in her eyes, as she was afraid to hear his answer. "Yeah, like a girlfriend."

He drew in a deep breath and looked past her to where he could see Sarah talking to Brad. Then he looked into her teary eyes.

"No…not really. I'm not ready for an exclusive relationship right now. My focus is on my new business and the renovations of the B&B."

Jill closed her eyes and whispered a silent thank you. When she opened her eyes she gave Travis a small smile. They stood looking at each other as if they were trying to let their emotions accept where their new relationship stood and move forward—as friends.

"Well, I did come over to talk to you with good intentions."

Travis smiled as he put his arm around her shoulders and guided her toward the porch swing at the B&B.

"Yeah, what's that?"

Jill continued to share her ideas. He pulled his phone out to store them on his note app.

"I love it! Hey, I don't know what's going on with your situation with Brad. But if you have some time this week, maybe we could meet with Jonah and discuss these ideas with him. He's in charge of the website."

"I'd like that."

Just then, Clara walked out from the main doors of the B&B. "I thought I heard chattering. It's nice to see you Jill."

"Hi, Clara. How are you?"

"I'm doing very well. Are you kids hungry? I made a big pot of spaghetti and meatballs for Brad, Sarah and the girls. You're welcome to eat with us."

Travis looked at Jill. "Yeah?"

She nodded her head. "Yeah, that sounds good. I'll go get the gang and let them know it's time to eat." She leaped off the swing, hopeful that life would go back to the way it used to be.

Jill and Travis sat around the table with everyone laughing and talking about her ideas of a fashion show competition. She noticed a change in Brad's mannerisms. He hardly talked directly toward her, it was always toward Sarah. This made her feel less important and somehow less obligated to his every need. It was nice to see that having his brace off made him be like his old self again.

Sarah liked her ideas and chimed in with her thoughts. "Hey, I just thought of a great idea! Well—actually two. One is to help raise money for the construction of the B&B and the other is a way to get exposure for Travis's dolls."

All eyes were on her as Travis was eager to hear how. "Yeah—what?"

"We can have a party here at the B&B with square/line dancing and auction off lunch date baskets!"

Travis shook his head with confusion. "What exactly is a lunch date basket?"

She stood from the table and walked around it.

"A lunch date basket is where anyone can make up a lunch and enter it to be auctioned off. And—whoever buys it gets a lunch date with the one who made it."

Travis's eyebrows drew close together and he felt confused. "And how are you going to expose my doll line?"

"We could set up a runway and have a run-through with live dolls. And display the dolls for purchase."

"Hmm! I like where you're going with this. So the auctioning off of lunch baskets will bring money in for the renovations, and the runway show will be the entertainment."

Sarah stopped behind his chair and put her hands on his shoulders. "Yes! Exactly!"

Her eyes looked upward as her hands laid on his shoulders and continued with a story from her past.

"I went to a hoedown once in Montana where they did the lunch basket auction. They had a live band with a square dance caller. My lunch basket sold for seventy-five dollars. It was a perfect night, dancing out under the stars..."

Tessa interrupted, "Did daddy buy your basket, Mommy?"

Sarah quickly looked over at her. "Yes, that is where we met." She then walked back to her chair which was beside Tessa and patted her daughter's knee.

Clara broke the silence. "That sounds like fun! I can get some of my quilter friends to donate quilts, table runners and other things to sell in the auction. And I'd betcha Bobby Sue and Greta would come up with some things to sell, too. Sarah, would you like to be in charge of the auction?"

"Um yes. I would love it."

Jill jumped in with her offer. "I can help with the runway show."

Brad cleared his throat. "I think I'll stick to the renovations."

Everyone was laughing and chatting among themselves when Greta and Jack walked into the room. "Can we join the party?"

Travis looked at his sister. "Sure. What are you two up to?"

Clara scooted out from the table. "Sit down, sit down. I'll go get you two a plate of spaghetti and meatballs."

Sarah jumped up. "I'll help you, Clara."

Greta and Jack sat down next to Travis, and Greta noticed Jill. Remembering the last time Jill was at the B&B when she'd broken her brother's heart. "Jill—what brings you here?"

Jill looked down at her utensils and fidgeted with them while thinking of what to say. She could feel the concern in Greta's tone of voice. "Um—I came to see Brad, and share with your brother an idea of how to create an interest in his doll collection."

"Really—so you're here on business—what's that?"

Travis could feel the tension rising. Knowing how protective his sister was of him, he butted in, "So, you never did tell me what you two are up to." Looking at Jack then back at Greta.

Greta took her stare off Jill and directed her response to her brother. "Back when I needed help mending the fences, you were in Tennessee; and now Mom and Dad are at the drill team competition in Texas. We just finished the last pasture near the pond."

Clara and Sarah walked into the room with their dinners. "There's plenty more if you want seconds." Clara offered. She then looked at Travis as she continued. "I'm going to make some calls to my quilter friends about what we were talking about. I'll catch up with you later."

Travis smiled. "Okay Grandma, sounds good. See you later."

He inquisitively looked at Brad. "Would you be up to meeting Jack and me in the morning on the back porch… say, around nine-thirty?'

"Yes, that sounds perfect. I'll have the blueprints with me." He looked from Travis to Jack, "So, is it just the two of you working on enclosing the porch tomorrow?"

Travis tilted his chair back onto two legs stretching out his arms, one toward Greta and the other toward Sarah. "Unless these girls don't have much to do tomorrow. We could always use extra hands."

Greta leaned over and poked his ribs causing him to drop his chair back down on all four legs. "Well, maybe. I have a group of kids from the orphanage coming tomorrow for a 10 o'clock lesson."

"Yeah, sure, I'll help." Sarah said as she stood and cued the girls to stand as well, and motioned them to mosey on out to the porch swing.

Jill felt uncomfortable with Greta's remark about Travis being in Tennessee. *So, he was in Tennessee…hmm, I suppose with Sabrina, again.* She scooted her chair out from the table and gave a half of a smile to Travis and told him she was going to spend some time with Sarah before leaving.

Travis shared with Greta and Jack the idea that Jill came up with—a competition for people to enter to win a free ticket to the live doll show to see their winning fabric designed on their chosen doll. This led to the next question Travis had wanted to ask Greta. "Would you be interested in writing bios for my dolls?"

Greta's eyes grew big. "Me?"

Travis smiled. "Yep. I was thinking of Jill, of course, as a career person. Sarah, as the mother of three, You, as a horse trainer and…" He looked at Jack, "Would you mind being interviewed as a ranch handler?"

Jack was caught by surprise. "Uh—I don't know. What actually is this for?"

Travis grinned. "Okay, this is what I'm thinking." He went on to explain that he was going to have a practice live runway show at the B&B's fundraiser as part of the entertainment, giving some good exposure to his doll line. A book telling the story about the dolls would help bring in some revenue.

Greta held her hand up and interrupted him. "Wait…you're having a fundraiser for the B&B with a live doll show?" Travis nodded his head. She then questioned. "And…who's going to be your live models?"

"I was thinking of you being a runway model, along with Jill, Sarah, and possibly Jack, with maybe the three girls and little Kendra. Sarah thinks we should have a lunch basket auction, too. Oh, and Grandma wants to get some of her friends to donate some of their quilting items to be auctioned off. So, what do you think?"

"Wow, I don't know—there's so much to think about, but from what I can comprehend, I think it sounds great—except the part about me writing peoples' stories."

"Aw, come on, Sis, you would be good at it."

Jack squirmed in his seat. "Uh, yeah, I'm not too sure about being a model."

Travis smiled, "Well, think on it. Don't say no yet."

Jack was quiet as they continued to talk about the whole ordeal. Telling his story was something he was not comfortable with. He and his twin brother, Jake, aged out of the orphanage a year ago. Bo was like the dad they never had. Growing up doing volunteer work at the farm taught them many skills, so when they needed a place to stay, Bo offered them a room and hired them as ranch handlers. He loved everything about being on the farm and enjoyed Greta's company too.

Chapter 17

Brad settled into his room at the barn, feeling confident being on his own with his new brace. Looking at his phone calendar, he noticed Wednesday night was the Alcoholics Anonymous course that he signed up for online. His mood changed from feeling good to feeling betrayed. That spiked punch at the after-party had really affected his choices. Then guilt started to set in as he remembered being a little too affectionate with Tara on the dance floor. His overreacting to Jill's being a no-show for their last performance caused him to drive recklessly. In turn, the resulting accident put him in a wheelchair and caused him to be fatherless in his future.

He was beside himself. As he tossed his phone on the bed, he felt emotional—wondering how to make it up to Tara for leading her on, knowing he blamed Jill for the accident, and now having feelings toward Sarah.

I can't believe how one night messed up my whole future. Why didn't someone warn me about the spiked punch? What do I do now? How can I make it up to Tara? What am I supposed to say to Jill? — 'Uh, sorry. I blamed you for over reacting and acting like an idiot because you were not at the show'. And then there's Sarah—sweet Sarah. I don't even deserve a chance with her with the way I've made a mess of my relationships with other girls. Who am I kidding? She probably has her eye on Travis. By the way she acted tonight— putting her hands on his shoulders—I'm pretty sure she does.

Sarah's and Jill's laughter caught his attention, so he pushed his wheelchair to the window to see what was going on outside. They were teaching the girls some cheer moves. He sat there with an involuntary smile as he watched the three girls try to coordinate clapping with the foot moves that Jill and Sarah were doing. Sitting there, he let his mood continue down the path of self-pity. *What kind of father would walk away from those girls? If he only knew how lucky he was to be a father. That's something I'll never get to experience now.* He closed the curtain and headed for the shower.

***

Jill plopped down on the ground. "Whew, your girls are wearing me out. I need a break."

Sarah joined her. "Right. Okay, girls we're done for the night. Why don't you head back to our room? And Tessa, you get your shower, then I'll be in to help Elise and Aubrey."

The girls ran toward the B&B as Jill watched. "They are so cute, but how do you keep up with them?

Sarah chuckled. "I don't know. Thankfully, I don't have a lot of free time to think about it. If I did, I think I would fall apart."

Jill nodded, and then changed the subject. "So, you seem to be hitting it off pretty well with Brad."

Sarah plucked a blade of grass as she acknowledged Jill's comment. "Uh, yeah I guess you could say that; he's easy to talk to."

"So are you interested in getting to know him better?"

Sarah stared at the blade of grass she was twiddling between her fingers. "Nah—I have my girls and that's all I need. And Travis is keeping me busy."

The mentioned of Travis's name made Jill feel uneasy about how little time she had spent with him since she took the summer job in Chicago, and how he was spending his time with Sabrina and now Sarah. "So—does Travis ever mention me while you're working with him?"

"Mmm…no not really."

Jill frowned. "Oh—do you think he's over me?"

Sarah tossed the grass blade and stood, wiping off the backside of her jeans. "I'm not sure what you're asking me. All I know is, he has been so busy around here that I don't think he's had much time to think or do anything else. Well, I better head into the B&B and get my girls cleaned up and tucked in bed."

"Okay. I should head on home too. I think it's time to head back to Chicago and finish out my summer assignment now that Brad is okay without me."

106

Chapter 18

The next morning Brad woke to the sound of neighing horses. "Huh?!" Tilting his head up, the early morning sunrise shining brightly through the window, he looked around and remembered where he was. Resting his head back onto his pillow, his thoughts were on Sarah and how he wanted to get to know her more. Clanging noises from behind the walls of his room caused him to get up and look out the doorway.

Bobby Sue was pushing the feed cart down the aisle, tossing the grain through the feed window of each stall. Then she would open each door to toss in the hay. As she turned the cart back toward the feed area she saw Brad. "Hey there, did you get moved in okay?"

Brad smiled with sleepy eyes. "Yes I did. I came last night."

Bobby Sue stopped the cart in front of him and smiled. "I see that maybe I woke you up?"

Nodding his head, he said. "Yeah, but I needed to get up. By the way, what time is it?"

"Oh, it's probably close to 7 by now."

"Well, I better get cleaned up. I'm supposed to meet Travis and Jack for breakfast so we can get started on the renovations today."

"Okay, that sounds good. Hey, if you see Sarah over at the B&B, can you let her know that I will have a new horse coming in today. If she wants to see him, tell her to bring the girls."

"I sure will." Brad was happy to have a reason to talk to Sarah and couldn't wait to run into her.

***

Travis and Jack were standing at the back porch when he wheeled his chair up to the ramp. "Oh good, someone is here to give me a boost onto the ramp. That's the first thing we need to fix so I can come in and out on my own."

Travis grabbed the handles to his wheelchair and pushed him up the ramp. "Now you see why my dad is not in charge of the renovations."

Jack chuckled under his breath and followed behind them. After they sat down at the dining room table, Brad laid the blueprints out in front of them as Sarah came in the room carrying a tray of muffins.

"Here you go boys, straight out of the oven."

Brad was the first to respond. "Wow, you cook too?"

She threw him a smirk as she tossed her hair out of her face. "You mean— bake?"

Travis perked up and reached for one of the chocolate chip muffins as she set the tray down. "Someone is spunky this morning."

"Well, I've been up since 6 o'clock baking and preparing breakfast for you guys."

Travis pulled a chair out beside him. "Here. Have a seat. Would you like a muffin?" He grabbed the tray of muffins and set them in front of her.

Brad chimed in. "Yeah, they're freshly baked."

She stood there and smirked looking at the two of them. Then she shook her head as she sat down beside Travis. "Okay, boss. Do you have a list made out yet as to what I'm doing today?"

"Well, actually we haven't gotten that far. But you can work alongside me today once we all have our breakfast."

"So are you guys ready for some egg and bacon casserole?"

They all nodded in agreement as she got up and headed for the kitchen.

Brad's eyes followed her out of the room, then remembered he was supposed to tell her about the new horse. He excused himself from the table and followed her into the kitchen.

Sarah was pulling the breakfast casserole out of the oven when he entered the room. "Did you need something?"

"Um, yeah. I was supposed to tell you that Bobby Sue is having a horse shipped here today and suggested you bring the girls to the barn to check him out."

She set the casserole down on a hot pad and acknowledged him with a nod of her head. She had been avoiding the barn as much as possible to keep her emotions in check. Everything about the facility brought up old painful feelings about Cole.

***

Jill texted Travis to see if he would be able to set up a meeting with herself and Jonah before she flew back to Chicago. He confirmed a time with Jonah and told her to meet at the B&B at lunchtime. She looked forward to spending time with him before leaving town.

She pulled up to the B&B and eagerly grabbed her briefcase out of the back seat and adjusted her silk scarf that matched her crop top. Walking toward the B&B she could hear Sarah squealing from the back porch area. Curious as to what was going on, she moseyed around to the back to see Sarah on the edge of the roof looking down at Travis.

"I can't do it! I can't."

Travis looked up at her from the bottom of the ladder. "Sarah you can do this! Hold onto the ladder and lower your legs down on the first rail. I'm holding the ladder."

"I'm afraid to lean over by only holding onto the ladder. Why is it so hard to come down? I didn't have a problem getting up on the roof."

"Okay, just sit tight, I have an idea." Travis turned around to see Jill standing there. "Hey, I didn't see you walk up. I have a situation that I'm trying to figure out here, so give me a minute or two."

Jill laughed as she looked up at Sarah. "What? Why in the world did you climb up there?"

Sarah pouted, "I don't want to talk about it. I just want down."

Travis came back with another extension ladder and propped it up beside the one Sarah was to climb down on. "Okay I'm going to climb up this ladder and help you climb out and over to your ladder."

Sarah's voice was shaky, "Are you sure this is going to work?"

As Travis climbed up his ladder Brad and Jill were intensely watching. "Jill, can you step on the bottom rail of Sarah's ladder while she swings herself onto it?"

Jill did as he asked without saying a word.

Once Travis reached Sarah, he smiled at her and reassured her that everything would be all right and she would be off the roof in no time.

"Okay, as you reach over and grab the top of your ladder I will put my arms around your waist and you lift off the roof to place your foot on the top rail. I won't let go of you until both feet are on the ladder. Then, you got it from there. Does that sound like a good plan?"

She had tears in her eyes as she whispered. "I feel like such a wimp. Thank you for being up here with me."

Jill and Brad started to cheer her on. "You've got this Sarah, come on down."

Once Sarah's feet landed on solid ground she hugged Jill. "Oh, I feel so stupid! I can't believe how I froze with fear!"

Brad wheeled his chair closer to her and reached out his hand to rub her arm in a consoling way. "Hey, glad to see you landed safely on the ground."

She sniffed as she wiped her eyes and withdrew from Jill's embrace. "Thanks. Brad. Me, too. I think I'll stick with you here on the ground and leave the high stuff to Travis and Jack."

Jill looked around. "Yeah—where's Jack?"

Brad hit his fist on the arm of his chair and with frustration said. "He went after more supplies. Man, I can't wait to get out of this wheelchair. I'm sorry, Sarah. You should never have gone on the roof. It should have been me up there."

"Whoa, wait—I went up there willingly. Neither you nor I had any idea that I would freeze like I did. Let's just forget it and move on." She offered Travis a hug and as he embraced her, she whispered, "Thank you so much. I'm sorry about freaking out."

He squeezed her tightly, rocking her back and forth. "It's over and now I know what not to ask you to do! So, why don't you make us some lunch?"

Jill jumped in, "Speaking of lunch—Can you let go of her now…so we can start our meeting?"

Travis chuckled as he released his hold on Sarah. "Yep, we need to get with Jonah and get this competition on the website."

Jill quickly grabbed Travis's arm and led him toward the door and away from Sarah. "See you later."

Sarah and Brad waved at them. Brad asked Sarah if she wanted help making the lunch.

"Sure, let me text Clara and have her send the girls to the kitchen to help, too."

Brad smiled and looked forward to spending time with Sarah, without Travis, and getting the chance to bond with her girls.

Chapter 19

Jill was looking at the fish Travis had added to his office aquarium when she heard a text come into his phone. He was in the closet collecting all the dolls that had been made so Jill could measure them for clothes patterns.

"Travis, you got a text…." Curious to see who it was from, she tapped the screen and saw it was from Sabrina. An immediate surge of huff came out of her mouth. Then she looked over at the closet and realized Travis hadn't heard her, so she tapped the screen again to read the first part of the text that appeared. "Hey Cowboy, when are we getting together again?"

With an armful of dolls, Travis rambled as he walked into the room. "Man, it's a mess in there. You would think a walk-in closet would give you enough room to put everything. I'm going to have to get Sarah to organize it for me and maybe hang some more shelves.

Jill turned his phone over to hide the bright screen and walked toward him. "Here, let me help carry some." She grabbed a few dolls and laid them on the table. "Wow, you've been busy. A little 6" doll caught her eye. "Aw, is this doll Kendra from the orphanage?" She asked as she held up the little blonde hair doll.

"Yep, that's Kendra. My mom is so attached to her. She's thinking of adoption."

"Really?" Jill stood looking at the small doll and tried to visualize herself adopting an orphan. *Could I commit myself to a child? Maybe…. Someday.*

"Hey, did you say something to me earlier?"

Jill laid the doll down and quickly remembered what she read on his phone. "Um, yeah. You got a text."

"I bet it was from Jonah. He should have been here by now." But before he reached his phone, Jonah walked in the room.

"There you are. I just got all the dolls out of the closet for Jill. She wants to get their measurements so she can design clothes for them."

They shook hands, and each grabbed a chair to sit at the table to start the meeting. Jill was relieved that Travis forgot about the text on his phone. At least for now his focus would be on her, and not on Sabrina.

***

The kitchen was full of laughter and chaos with the girls helping prepare lunch. Brad loved being around the girls. They were full of energy and eager to help.

Sarah was in command mode. "Okay. Listen up, girls. We are going to make individual sloppy joe muffins using refrigerator muffins. So who wants to make the sloppy joes, and who wants to get the muffin pan out and coat it with oil, then add the dough to each holder?"

The two oldest jumped, waving their arms in the air. "I do; I do."

"Okay, good. Tessa, I will give you the recipe card and you can start gathering all your ingredients while Elise prepares the muffin pan. Aubrey, you and Brad can help me make the spinach salad. Does that sound okay to everyone?"

They happily agreed and scrambled to grab their items to start.

"Oh, wait! Line up to wash your hands and I'll find you each an apron to wear."

Brad lifted his eye brow and expressed his thought on the apron idea. "Um…. I think I'll pass on wearing one."

Sarah paused as she was tying one on Aubrey. "Aw, are you sure? You would look charming wearing one."

Aubrey pleaded, "Come on, it will be fun to dress like a chef." She continued to look at him with pleading puppy eyes.

"Okay, how can I say no to you?"

Aubrey hugged him the best way she could with him being in a wheelchair. "Yay!"

Sarah smirked as she tossed an apron on his lap. He lifted his chin up toward her as a way of accepting the apron. Aubrey helped him put it on and was ready for her salad assignment.

***

Jill kept an intense eye on the time. She had to fly back to Chicago by seven o'clock, but wanted to have everything in order to launch the design competition. Jonah was a great asset in implementing her ideas to the website. Now all she wanted to do was finish out her summer assignment in Chicago so she could get back to Ohio with hopes of reconnecting with Travis. Shutting her briefcase, she concluded their meeting.

Travis offered her a hug. "Thank you for coming with your idea. I'm sure it will help get exposure for my doll collection."

Taking in a deep breath, Jill didn't want to let go of his embrace or the smell of his presence mixed with cologne. "You're welcome. I hope to be able to come back before the event to fit the outfits on the live dolls before it actually starts."

"Yes, that would be great. We'll keep in touch. Hey listen…" he released his embrace. "I better let you go. I don't want you to miss your flight."

She held her smile as she looked up at him, wishing she didn't have to leave. Then she nodded in agreement and walked out the door.

Travis had a pleasant expression on his face until a text chimed in. He noticed as he looked at it that he had missed Sabrina's text earlier. She was texting him again.

Hey Cowboy, you must be very busy. It's been hard for me to talk with you when you don't return my calls or respond to my text. What's up? Luv, Sabrina

Holding his phone in his hand, he wondered why he felt so good when he was with her, but when he wasn't around her, he hardly thought of her. He stuffed his phone in his pocket with good intentions to talk with her after Jonah left.

***

Sarah texted Clara to tell her lunch was ready. Then she texted Travis to see if he was finished with his meeting and could join them for lunch. The girls were proud of their lunch display. On a platter they arranged their sloppy joe muffins in a shape of a wreath. Then they added chips and Fritos with dip in a glass bowl in the center of it. Aubrey and Brad made a spinach salad and a fruit bowl. Clara and Joe walked in and saw the girls' display and praised them for a job well done. Sarah was all smiles as she looked around the kitchen. She and her girls were in a good place, and she wasn't thinking about what tomorrow would bring.

Brad wheeled his wheelchair over to the table with plates on his lap and caught a glimpse of Sarah's smile. *She is so radiant, Lord. I would be honored if you would allow me to build a relationship with her.*

Bobby Sue walked into the kitchen. "Mmm… something smells good."

Travis walked in behind her. "Hey! You're back! When did you get home?"

"Late last night."

Grabbing a plate for her from the cupboard, Sarah suggested she stay and eat with them.

"Thank you, I think I will. By the way, did Brad tell you that I have a new horse coming in today?"

Sarah nodded as she glanced over at Brad. "Yes he did. What's the horse's story?"

Bobby Sue sat down at the table along with everyone else and offered to pray for the meal before telling the story of how and why she bought the horse.

"Well, I really wasn't looking to buy one, but something about this horse's spirit spoke to me."

Aubrey questioned her. "The horse talked to you?"

Everyone giggled, then Tessa spoke-up, "No silly, horses don't talk."

Bobby Sue smiled and nodded her head slightly. "Well now, I'd have to say this one talked to me…."

The girls stared intensely at her as she continued. "You see, he may not have used our words, but he used horse language."

Elise asked. "What did he say?"

"He told me he was sad, and didn't have a purpose any longer."

Everyone was quiet while Bobby Sue took a drink of lemonade, then continued. "So I thought about it the whole weekend while I was at the ranch with the drill team, and I visited him a couple times a day. I caressed his head and neck, and his response is what touched my heart. He would lower his head more and more into my arms so that the weight of his head lay in my arms." She paused and looked up to the ceiling then back down at the three girls. "Someone inside my heart told me to bring him home to the ranch."

Aubrey's eyes were wide as she asked who.

Elise elbowed her and whispered, "You know—the One she prays to. He's the one who has those angels we learned about. They're everywhere."

Sarah overheard Elise whispering and thought back to when the girls made snow angels with Jill while they were snowed in at the diner. This is where they first met her in New York, and when Jill told the girls that there were angels all around.

Aubrey stared at nothing then looked up at Bobby Sue as if she believed she was an angel saving this horse's life. "Can we see him?"

"Yes, I would love for you girls to come see him. He should be here before sunset."

Tessa was excited and wanted to know more about him. "Does he have a name?"

"He does, but I was thinking we could give him a new name to fit his new life. So what do you say that you girls get to know him and give me your ideas of what to name him?"

They were all for it. Sarah smiled at the opportunity for the girls to have a horse to love on. She felt it was kind of ironic that this lonely horse found a home at the same place as she did when feeling alone.

Clara and Joe walked in the room carrying boxes full of different baskets and apologized for being late for lunch. "Look what we found in the shed…" Greta and Jack lingered in behind them with more boxes of baskets and Clara continued her sentence with enthusiasm, "A whole bunch of woven baskets to use for the lunch box auction!"

Sarah quickly got up from the table and grabbed a few more plates as the girls asked to be excused. They wanted to dig into the boxes to see which basket they wanted to use. The rest of them sat around the table talking among themselves about the fundraiser, trying to catch Bobby Sue up to date on everything.

Chapter 20

Brad heard a diesel truck rumble by his window and wondered if it was the arrival of Bobby Sue's new horse. Knowing Sarah and the girls would be anxiously waiting, he unlocked the brakes on his wheelchair and eagerly pushed himself toward the door. Out in the aisle stood the three girls with carrots and apples in their hands. Looking around he didn't see Sarah. *Hmm—I wonder where she is.*

Sarah was pulling baskets from the boxes Clara brought and arranging them on the kitchen counter. She told her that she would wash them up. This gave her a good excuse to send the girls to the barn to meet the new horse without her.

She heard the diesel engine, and it sent her thoughts back in time. Flashes of a red pick-up truck pulling a horse trailer went through her vision.

Oh Cole, Is it really our truck? We can now travel all over doing what we love to do!

She remembered Cole surprising her with a horse that came with the trailer. He said that the owner told him he couldn't leave the horse behind. This horse became Cole's new rodeo horse. It was a Palomino Paint with distinctive markings. On his forehead was a white heart shape under his forelock and a small round spot under his belly close to the girth area. The rest of his body was golden with a white tail and mane. His dark eyes and black muzzle drew you into his space and made you want to love on him.

Tears rolled down her cheeks.

"Sarah…."

She jumped at the sound of her name. "Uh—What!?" Turning around, she saw Brad in his wheelchair. "Oh, you scared me. I was—um, I guess I was in my own world." She turned her head away from him and wiped away her falling tears, hoping he had not already noticed them. She planted a fake smile on before turning back around to ask, "Did you need something?"

He wheeled his chair closer to her with an inquisitive expression as he reached for her hand. "Are you okay?'

Involuntarily she gave him her hand and sat on his lap. "Oh give me a minute." She swallowed hard, looking around for something to drink, then realized that she was sitting on his lap. "Oh—I'm sorry. I didn't mean to sit on your lap." Their eyes locked. He could see that she'd been crying. She motioned to stand, but he put his arms around her waist encouraging her to stay. Feeling her in his arms, he wanted to lean in and kiss her. There was an electrical attraction between them, but he knew it wasn't the right time.

He reassured her as he rubbed her lower back. "It's okay. I'm fine. Sit here."

"But what about your…"

"Really, I'm fine. It doesn't hurt. I thought you would have been at the barn with the girls to see the new horse. Are you sure everything is alright?"

Just then her oldest daughter came bursting into the kitchen. "Mommy! Mommy! The horse—he looks just like Daddy's horse! Come and see."

Sarah immediately stood and clenched her teeth. "What?!" Panic started to pound within her chest.

Tessa excitedly told her that it was a yellow horse and that he ate the carrots that she offered him.

Drawing in a deep breath, she composed herself and went into Mommy mode. "Tessa, I'm not able to come right now. I told Clara I would wash all the baskets. But you run along and enjoy spending time with the horse and then you can tell me all about it tonight at bedtime."

Tessa nodded than looked at Brad. "Do you wanna come see the horse?"

Brad smiled at her. "Heck, yeah, I want to see the horse." He followed her out of the kitchen, sensing that Sarah needed time to herself.

As soon as they left the room Sarah gripped her stomach and tears poured out involuntarily. Grabbing the nearest chair, she sat with her head in her arms on the table and sobbed. Hearing the words 'Daddy's horse' from her daughter gave her a quick, jabbing hope of Cole and his horse actually being in the barn. She continued to create images of herself working in the kitchen while Cole was out in the barn with their girls showing them how to ride a horse. They would all walk in together when she called them for dinner. She sniffed as she lifted her head to grab a napkin out of the basket at the center of the table.

"Where are those angels now…huh, where?" She blew her nose, then grabbed a few more napkins to wipe her eyes. She felt drained. Resting her head back on the table she continued to weep softly until she fell asleep.

Later, Brad wheeled his chair into the kitchen and saw that she was sleeping. His frustration rose, and he wished he could pick her up and carry her to her room. Determination welled up inside of him to do whatever it would take to speed his recovery and walk again. He had a new focus—Sarah. Backing out of the room he reached for the light switch and knocked a cookie sheet off the counter.

She lifted her head in a startled motion. "Uh, what's going on?"

Brad whirled his chair around with an apologetic look. "I'm so sorry! I saw that you were asleep so I thought I would quietly turn the lights off and leave. I accidentally knocked the pan off the counter."

Looking at it on the floor, she picked it up. As she turned around she saw the pile of baskets. "Oh, that's okay. I need to finish cleaning the baskets."

"Do you want help?"

Still a little disoriented, she nodded as she rubbed her swollen eyelids, "Are you sure you don't mind?"

"Yeah, I'm sure. I just left the girls. They are hand grazing and brushing the new horse on the hillside."

Sadness came over her face. "Okay. Actually I would like the company. Thanks." She knew she needed to pull herself back into reality and move onward. This is her new life and she needed to remind herself again that she would never have Cole.

***

Brad was sitting at his desk, trying to focus on the blueprint to close in the back porch of the B&B when he heard thunder. He wheeled his chair over to the window and watched sheets of rain falling as the sky darkened, then lightened again with flashes of lightening. Leaving Sarah earlier that evening left him feeling down, and the pressure of the storm over the ranch added to the stillness of his unknown future.

The sound of the screen door banging from the back porch caught his attention.

Oh boy, I better latch the door or it's going to be torn off with this wind. He wheeled himself down the hall and opened the door to grab the swinging screen door. With the wind and rain blowing, he held his head down and reached for the flapping door. Finally, he leaned forward to get a good grip on the door handle. A strong gust of wind jerked the door off the hinges and out of his hand. It caused him to lose his balance and fall out of his chair. Lightening flashed and thunder sounded as he scrambled to get on his knees to pull himself back into his wheelchair. But the screen door was over him and jammed against his chair. His hip brace was caught in the lattice trim on the screen door. Frustrated and a little panicked, he tried to roll back and forth to get loose of the door. Suddenly a bright light came on. He went still and looked up, wondering why it was so bright. There stood Sarah under the porch light with a frightened look and eyes wide.

"What happened?"

"Never mind what happened. Can you get this door off me and help me get in my chair?

Sarah immediately pulled the chair back and lifted the screen door, tugging until it came loose from his brace. She wiped the rain off her face and she reached for his hand to help him up. He was drenched with rain, making it hard to hold onto him. She tugged his body as much as she could, but because he was all the way down he was dead weight. She couldn't budge him.

"I can't lift you!" She yelled over the sounds of the storm. Then she looked around for a way to help him and spotted the built-in bench seat. "Can you pull yourself over to the bench?"

He nodded his head "I think so."

Scooting himself toward the bench, he used his upper strength to lift his torso, and she put her arms around his waist to help lift him. He could feel her heart beating against his back. His adrenaline surged and with all his strength he lifted his lower body onto the bench. Out of breath and soaked to the bones, they sat with their heads resting against each other. The storm started to let up and the wind calmed down. Once their breathing was back to normal, they looked at each other with passion. There was a physical attraction between them as their bodies drew closer. He gently pulled her into him, wrapping his arms around her willingness. She held on tightly, laying her head on his shoulder while tears rolled down her cheeks. Mixed emotions were fighting for her attention. Warmth, tenderness, passion—guarded, questioning, guilt. She quickly pulled away and turned her head to hide her tears.

Brad didn't want to let go of what he was feeling for her, but he could see that he needed to change the mood. And he wasn't too sure what was going on in her head. Physically he felt her willingness to be held by him.

"Hey—thanks for saving me from being attacked by a screen door…."

She looked at him with a smile. "My pleasure. The next time you feel like taking on a storm door make sure you have backup."

He chuckled. "Uh—yeah. I owe you—again—someday.

They held a smile. He softly asked, "Maybe we can keep this as our little secret?"

She smirked. "Or blackmail."

Standing, Sarah reached for his hand. "Come on. Let's get you in your chair so we can both go in and get dry."

Trying to control her emotions, she made a conscious awareness of her body space as she helped him into his chair.

Chapter 21

Sarah woke to the sound of backing beepers. Sitting up quickly with her heart pounding, she looked around the room and saw she was alone. She grabbed her phone and she wondered what time it was, and where her girls were. Her phone showed the time as nine-thirty. She flung the covers off and jumped toward the window. There she saw a pile of lumber and Jack's truck.

They must be getting ready to work on the porch. Oh man! Where are the girls?

Sarah hurriedly dressed, pulled her hair into a ponytail, and scurried out the door.

Clara was in the hallway when Sarah approached her with a worried look on her face. "Where ya going in such a hurry?"

"Oh, I overslept, and I feel so disoriented. I don't know where the girls are and…."

Clara reached her arm out to console her. "Now, now. The girls are fine. I saw them this morning in the kitchen. They told me that they were too excited to sleep and went to the barn. They wanted to be there when Bobby Sue fed the new horse."

Sarah breathed deep, trying to slow her racing mind. "Okay, I'd better make some breakfast for them."

Clara tried to calm her. "They grabbed a granola bar and an apple before heading to the barn. They're fine. I'm surprised you're getting started so late. Did the storm keep you up?"

She thought back to when she was wakened with a loud noise and discovered Brad on the porch floor trapped under the screen door. Images of their embrace in wet clothes as she helped him to the bench—and of his pulling her into a hug as sheets of rain blew over them. A sudden rush of cold chills ran up her body.

Rubbing her arms, she answered Clara. "Yeah, I guess so."

She wasn't sure how much she should tell her, or anyone, about last night. "Did you hear anything last night?"

Clara smiled. "Honey, I didn't hear a thing. When I got up to feed the cat, I saw that the screen door was off, and the cat bowls were out in the yard. I thought it must have been a heck of a storm."

Sarah nodded as she said under her breath. "Yes, one I'll never forget."

***

Brad started checking in the materials that were delivered when Travis, Jack, and his brother Jake, pulled up. He had spent a restless night with shooting pain around his left hip. With great concern, he'd left a message for his doctor to see if he could get in right away to have it looked at. He yawned, waved at the guys, and wondered if Sarah would keep her distance from him after he pulled her into his arms last night. The passion he felt for her was so unexpected. But because she pulled away from his embrace, he worried whether she would want to be around him today.

Looking around, Travis was amazed at what a small storm cell on the radar had caused the night before. Tree branches on the ground…trash cans in the parking area…and then he noticed the storm door was missing. "Wow, I didn't think the storm was that intense."

Brad wheeled his chair over to where Travis stood. "Yeah. It may have been a quick storm, but it had a big punch to it. Look, it tore off the storm door."

"I see that. Man, I'm glad no one was out on the porch when that happened."

Brad kept quiet. He didn't feel it was necessary to share what happened during the storm. He was just concerned with what Sarah was feeling toward him.

Travis asked Jack if he would check the screen door to see if it needed any repairs and re-hang it. Then he asked his brother to remove all the dead tree branches and take them to the burn pile. The brothers took to their assignments right away.

Travis looked at Brad. "Have you had breakfast yet?"

"Actually, I haven't. The storm kept me up last night and so did my hip. I have a call in to my doctor to make sure everything is still healing the way it's supposed to."

"Really? Maybe the storm caused the flare-up. I've heard that people who have rods and pins in them are affected by the weather."

Not wanting to share the details about what happened on the porch last night with Sarah and the storm door, he simply agreed with Travis's theory. "Yep, I'm sure the storm had something to do with it."

"Well listen, why don't you go to the kitchen and grab something to eat. Then fill the water cooler and bring it out. It's going to be a humid day today. Jack and Jake will modify the ramp before framing in the porch."

Brad was glad to hear about the modification of the ramp; he nodded and turned his chair toward the door.

"So, one last lift onto the ramp?"

Travis chuckled as he reached for the handles of his chair, "Let's hope so."

***

Sarah was finishing her breakfast when Brad wheeled himself into the kitchen. Her eyes met his with a surprising look. This late in the morning she didn't think she would run into him. She felt like they had had a secret fling last night. She was embracing him in the rain with nothing but clinging, wet clothes between them as she'd tried to lift him onto the bench. And the hug he offered her after the frantic energy of the storm ceased made her realize she hadn't embraced anyone like that except Cole. Her feelings this morning left her feeling guilty.

Brad lifted his eyebrows and gave her a half smile, sensing that she was not comfortable seeing him. To break the silence, he said softly. "Hey."

She looked down at her plate as she responded, "Hi. Can I help you with something?"

His smile grew bigger and he continued to wheel himself closer to the table. "No, you helped me enough last night. I'm just going to grab a yogurt from the fridge and a banana, and I'll be out of your way."

Scooting her chair away from the table she went to the silverware drawer and grabbed a spoon. "Here—you'll need this."

Their hands touched as he took the spoon from her hand. Her eyes softened and a smile lifted slightly from her lips. "Do you need anything else?"

Wanting to stay in her presence, he looked around and then remembered that he needed to fill a cooler with water. "Uh, yeah—if you're sure you don't mind. I need to get a drinking cooler and fill it for the crew today."

Sarah let herself be in the moment and not in her head. "Okay. I can help you with that."

Brad's phone buzzed with a call. He looked to see who it was. He held up his finger; it was from his doctor's office. "I have to take this call."

Sarah nodded.

"Hello?"

Brad continued talking to the nurse about getting an appointment to have the doctor check his hip.

Sarah was listening to his conversation while getting the cooler out of the closet and felt concerned. She heard him say that after he had fallen out of his chair, he had some needle-like twinges in his left hip and they lingered throughout the night. Before he ended the call, he repeated his scheduled appointment for later that day—3:30 pm.

Sarah immediately asked. "I just heard you making a doctor's appointment. Do you think you messed up something in your hip last night?"

As he put his phone back into his pocket, he tried not to sound too concerned. "Let's hope not. The pain is easing, but I think I should still have it checked out." Looking at the water cooler, he asked her if she would put it on his foot rest to take to the job site. He was eager to get to work since he had to leave to see the doctor later.

Sarah carried the cooler over to his chair and set it where he asked. She felt a surge of blood pumping as an awareness of being in close proximity to him. Taking in a deep breath—filling herself with his cologne caused her to pause in the moment. Closing her eyes, she couldn't let go of the handles on the cooler.

Brad leaned in closer and put his hands on top of hers to adjust the cooler to a position where he felt it wouldn't fall.

Blood rushed to her head, and she felt very vulnerable as her body wanted to draw closer to him…like a magnet. The pull was so strong that it took all her might to fight her desire to pull him close and kiss him. Trying to shake the image of him hugging her the night before, she pulled her hands from under his and backed away from his chair. The same surge of desire lingered in the room. Brad felt the same pull, but finally, after seconds passed, he thanked her and wheeled himself out of the room.

She watched him leave. Confused that she was so drawn to him, she questioned herself. *What's happening to me? Am. I. Able. To let go of Cole? No, no. I can't go there! It's not right! What about the girls?*

Book club questions for discussion.   Chapters 10-21

❖ *Have you ever made your own assumptions on why things happened the way they did in your life, as Jill did in Chapter 10? When Jill learned about Brad's sterility, she immediately related it to herself and is now contemplating whether she is supposed to be with Brad.*

❖ *Have you ever wanted a relationship to work out so much that you ignored signs that the other person was not as into you as much as you were with them? How did you handle the aftermath?*

❖ *Chapter 15 expresses the impulsive decisions Jill made about taking a summer job without thinking of her commitments with Travis and how it would affect others. Have you ever made an impulsive decision in your life? If so, how did it affect others in a positive or negative way?*

❖ *In Chapter 17, when Brad reflected on how he acted under the influence of alcohol, he knew he had to humble himself and apologize for his wrongdoings. Do you think people who abuse others while under the influence of a substance recognize their wrong doings? If they do recognize it, but don't humble themselves to right their wrongs, what are they lacking?*

❖ *What are ways to share with others about methods to avoid substance abuse?*

Book club questions for discussion.   Chapters 10-21

❖ *Music and song lyrics have a way of touching our emotions. Are you conscious that what you hear may be influencing your emotions?*

Chapter 22

Tessa was brushing the new horse's mane when Travis walked into the barn. Elise and Aubrey were rearranging the tack box that Bobby Sue had assigned to the horse.

"I see you girls are taking good care of our new fella."

Tessa proudly said, "Yep. Are you here to test drive him?"

Travis chuckled, "Yeah, I guess you could say that."

Bobby Sue walked out of the tack room carrying an Austrian saddle and smiled when she saw Travis. She had asked him to ride the new horse so she could evaluate him from the ground.

"Hey, Mom."

"Hi. Are you ready for this?"

Travis grinned. "It's been a while since I've had to run a horse through your evaluation course. But yeah, I'm ready."

He looked the horse over. Then he rubbed his hands across both sides of the horse to see if he was sore or misaligned. He continued down each leg, giving the horse a sense of Travis's gentle touch and vulnerability. Trust had to start from the ground before he would mount the horse and ride him through the rest of the evaluation.

Tessa stepped back and watched with her sisters as Travis continued to work. The horse responded very well with his command. Travis lifted each hoof one at a time, then placed them back down with control and ease. This showed that the horse was handled with respect in his past. He continued to rub his neck up to his jaw bone as he softly talked to the horse. Again, the horse was very responsive, keeping his ears attentive to him. Rubbing his muzzle, Travis worked his thumb into his mouth and applied some pressure to the space in his mouth where the bit sets. The horse willingly opened his jaw. Travis rubbed the sides of his teeth. He felt a few sharp points but no sores on the gums. The final test was for Travis to grab the horse's tongue and hold it out to the side of his mouth. This showed submission from the horse if he allowed him to do it without a lot of head fight. Travis let go of his tongue with an approving nod of his head. The horse had a good disposition.

Bobby Sue let out a sigh of relief followed by a smile. "Well done."

Tessa squeezed the brush she held during the evaluation and asked. "Did he pass?"

Travis smiled. "He passed."

The girls squealed and clapped their hands.

"Now it's time to tack him up and see how he is under saddle," Bobby Sue said, as she tossed the saddle pad on his back, then the saddle. Once the horse was tacked, they followed him out to the arena as Travis led the way.

***

Back in the kitchen Sarah realized that Brad forgot to take drinking cups out for the crew. She quickly grabbed a stack of cups and headed toward the back porch.

Travis had the new horse on a lunge line directing him to pick up his right lead as he was cueing him to move forward. The horse felt frisky and gave a whinny, bucking around at the end of the lead line.

Sarah quickly looked over at the outdoor arena and saw the palomino flying around. She stopped and watched the horse running around and around in circles as Travis controlled the circumference of its circle. Her heart was drawn to the image of the horse's natural ability to run with restrictions to no set destination. She continued to stare, and her heart seemed to weep with the understanding of her heart beating without love. Shaking her thoughts away, she quickly went over and placed the cups on the table next to the water cooler.

Without being noticed, she walked toward the stillness of the pond, wanting it to comfort her. Stopping along the way she let her feelings reflect with the sights and sounds of nature.

She saw two large rocks pressed tightly against each other on the ground. One was dark with the other light in color, and between them was one small wildflower standing strong. As she stared at the odd grouping, she compared them with the pressure in her life. The dark rock represented her past and the light grey one represented her unknown future. Then she noticed the wildflower. Although delicate, it had enough inner strength to push up between the two large rocks and produce the beautiful yellow blossoms that hung from it.

Tears of pressure poured out of her as she gave into letting her emotions flow without holding them in.

Continuing on toward the pond, she noticed a pile of thin dead tree branches all intertwined with the green ground covering around it. Reflecting on the image, she saw her confused thoughts in a tangled mess within her own life—not wanting to let go of the past, but forced to live out each day in her present situation.

Arriving at the edge of the pond she saw her reflection as a water plant. It was visually under water with the top of it stretching to pierce out of the water to avoid drowning. With Cole no longer in her life, she stretched herself to carry on for the sake of her girls, trying not to suffocate in self-pity.

A water bug spinning around and around caught her attention. Walking closer she studied it as it aimlessly spun, making a whirlpool around itself.

She thought to herself. *This is me. Just like the horse, and this water bug, I'm going around and around stuck in my own sorrow, heading nowhere.*

Glancing up to the sky, she wondered if God was real and why she couldn't move on from a life without Cole. Then she saw a sign of hope. A large pine tree up on the hillside with its branches stretched out with new shoots facing upward. She walked eagerly toward the fresh scent of pine needles and felt her spirit lift. Suddenly, she stopped in her tracks when she saw a dark hole within the branches. "Uh. That's me!"

Her spirit began to feel glum again and she stared at the hole in the center of the tree. Backing away with a gesture of her hand as if she were pushing it away, she looked up and called out a plea, "If You are real, please help me. Heal me of my broken heart."

She then looked down her arm and toward her out-stretched fingers, and saw the hole was surrounded by dark green limbs. It wasn't alone.

The older branches were longer and stronger at the trunk of the tree, and she looked up from there and saw all the branches full of pine needles facing upward, shaping the tree to funnel her gaze to look up to the Creator of the tree.

She walked closer to study the branches with brown pine needles that were closer to the tree itself. She concluded that as the tree aged, with maturity each branch grew in strength and length with new growth of greenery. Her past may be dead and gone, but if she looked to the Creator, He would supply her with her surrounding sources, to grow new beginnings, and to flourish like the continuously fragrant evergreen tree.

Sarah had a new breath of fresh air in her lungs as she walked back to the B&B and a new perspective on her life. She smiled and felt a small piece of contentment that was placed in her during this walk of soul searching.

Chapter 23

Clara and Joe were bustling around in the kitchen when Sarah strolled in with her three girls.

Clara smiled, "Good morning my little sleepyheads."

The girls walked toward Clara to hug her. Sarah smiled and went straight toward the coffee pot, then greeted them. "Good morning Clara, Joe. Are you going to church this morning?"

Joe perked up, and replied, "Yes, we are. And you?"

Up until now Sarah had never had the desire to go to church. But after her soul-searching walk with nature, something gave her the desire to go. "You know, I think I would like to go with you guys. What time does it start?"

Joe smiled, "Well, we go to the first service at 9:30 and there is another one at 11:00. Whichever one you want to go to, we will take you."

"Um, well—since we are up and getting our breakfast we could probably go to the 9:30 service. What time do we have to leave?"

Clara spoke up, "Ten minutes after nine. That way I can introduce you and the girls to the leader of the children's ministry. They have a wonderful program for the kids."

"Okay. Well, we'll finish up here and meet you on the porch when we're ready."

***

Sarah was surprised with the atmosphere of the church. The contemporary worship music flowing through the speakers in the church lobby was also playing in the parking lot. People of all ages were smiling, chatting, and wearing casual clothing. She noticed they had a coffee shop with a book store right beside it, and an area where you could sit around small tables. There were big screen monitors mounted everywhere.

Clara directed them toward the check-in station for the girls to be signed in and directed toward their age-appropriate classes. Once the stickers were printed, they put them on each of the girls and one on Sarah, too. They had the same ID number on each of the stickers.

Clara explained, "Now, you're the only one who can go back in the children's section and pick up the girls when it's over. This is our child security system."

The children's leader came over, introduced herself and offered her a tour of the area. Sarah nodded, and they all followed behind her. After the tour she stooped down and kissed the girls good-bye and told them to be on their best behavior. They agreed and couldn't wait to go to their classes. It had been several months since they had interacted with kids their own age after moving to New York and now to the B&B.

The auditorium was breathtaking, not only with the size of the room, but also the colors and lighting.

Sarah flipped through the bulletin that she had received as she'd walked in. They had a list of classes and information about them with their locations and times. Another section listed upcoming events. The back of the bulletin had the title of the sermon—Our Personal Responsibility.

Underneath the title were verses:

Romans 10: 8,9,10: But what does it say? "The Word is near you. It is in your mouth and in your heart, that is, the word of faith we are proclaiming: That if you confess with your mouth, "Jesus is Lord," and believe in your heart that God raised Him from the dead, you will be saved. For it is with your heart that you believe and are justified, and it is with your mouth that you confess and are saved.

Looking on down the paper were a few lines to write notes about the chapter he was teaching from: Romans 12.

The lights dimmed, and the live music started playing. The worship leader approached the front of the stage, welcoming everyone, and started leading the congregation in singing the words that were projected on the monitors.

Sarah looked around, hoping she would see Brad. She hadn't seen him since he went to the doctor to check out the twinges in his hip. She had thought about him all night and looked forward to seeing him again.

It was hard for her to focus on the words to the songs, as she had never heard them before. Her eyes roamed the room, and she noticed most of the people were singing, and some even had their hands lifted in an up position. She stared at the girl closest to her and watched her sway back and forth looking so peaceful, with the rhythm of the music.

She thought to herself, *Could I be like her someday, and really trust in You, Lord? I just don't know You. But I see in this room so many are singing songs about You and have a joyful look on their faces. I want to know You, Lord.*

Just then the song ended, and the worship leader announced that he felt led to sing one more song. It was called, 'I want to know You'.

As the words were flashed on the monitor she looked around thinking, *Was I talking out loud? Did He hear what I said? I can't believe they have a song saying, 'I want to know You'.*

She began to read the words on the monitor as they sang. Tears started to form in her eyes, and a yearning desire was building up in her. Sarah listened to the music as she read the words out loud. The chorus played over and over "I want to know You. Let Your Spirit overwhelm me. Let your presence overtake my heart." Rocking to the music with her eyes closed, she felt the tears run down her cheeks.

She whispered, "I want a relationship with You, Lord. Help me find my way to You."

After church Joe offered to take them to lunch. The girls were excited to go out to eat. They enjoyed being with Clara and Joe as if they were their true grandparents.

Chapter 24

Travis was in Brad's office on the first floor of the B&B when Sarah heard construction noise and saw Brad's door open. With a full smile on her face, she picked up her pace and walked closer to his room. She was excited to see Brad. It had been a while since he was at the B&B.

She abruptly stopped at his doorway when she saw Travis in the room. "Oh, it's you."

Travis turned toward the door and chuckled. He attempted to talk over the construction noise as he questioned her, "Uh, yeah. Who were you hoping it would be?"

Sarah's lips pressed together as she could feel the embarrassment creeping into her expression. "Well—I assumed it was going to be Brad. It's his office, correct?" Before he could answer her, she looked around and saw a crew reconstructing the bathroom.

Travis smiled. "Well, yeah it's his office. But, he's not going to be here for a while. So they are making the bathroom handicapped accessible while he's gone. I'm…"

Sarah's mouth drooped along with her shoulders and she interrupted, "So, he did mess up his hip during the fall the other night."

Travis snapped his head toward her in disbelief. "What? When did he fall? He didn't mention anything to me about it."

"He didn't? Hmm. Well, I heard him say he had twinges in his hip the other day when his doctor's office called him. And…"

Travis continued her sentence. "Yeah, he did mention that. I assumed it was from all the rods, plates and screws he has in him. I even told him that. But—he didn't say a word about falling."

Sarah wanted to change the subject before he realized he didn't get an answer to his question. She glanced down at the mail she had in her hand. "Oh, here. I got the mail. I was coming to drop it off to Brad."

Travis thanked her as she handed him the mail. His phone buzzed while he was flipping through the mail. He looked at his phone and was eager to answer it. "Oh, it's the County Engineer's office. I need to take this call and set up the inspection for the electrical updates." He lifted the phone to his ear as Sarah waved and left the room.

She was relieved Brad didn't mention to Travis about what happened between them the night of the storm. But she was disappointed in not seeing him and wondered how soon he would be back to work.

Walking into the kitchen she saw Clara and Greta pulling stems off a cluster of grapes. "Can I help?" She asked.

Greta got up and gestured for her to sit in her seat. "Yes, perfect timing. I have to put some time on the new horse. By the way, I need to get with you sometime and get your story—the one you would want to go with the doll Travis is making."

"Making?" Sarah looked puzzled.

"Yes, my brother wants me to write a story on each of his dolls. Well at least the ones who will be represented by a live doll model. And he picked you as the rodeo/barrel racer doll. Didn't he talk to you about it?"

Sarah frowned, "No, he didn't." Then her mind raced. *Oh, I don't want to share my story with her, let alone have it out there for the world to read. No. I can't. I won't do it. But how am I going to get out of it?*

Greta continued, "Oh, well. I guess you might want to talk to him to make sure I understood him correctly. In the meantime, you can help Grandma stem the grapes. She's going to make grape jelly to sell at the fund raiser."

Sarah was a bit relieved for the moment. "Okay. That I can do." She turned and looked at Clara. "I would love to help you."

Clara smiled, "Okay! You know it won't be long before we have our big event. Joe is working with Jack and his brother to make the runway ramp."

Sarah needed to confide in her about not wanting to tell her story. "About the runway show—and me being a live model— I don't want to share my story."

Clara nodded. "I would have to agree with you about the story books. I think I need to talk to Travis about it—and see if he would put that on hold. We need to work on the rest of the fund raiser ideas first. It will be here before you know it."

Sarah smiled. She loved that Clara understood where she was coming from without insisting on knowing her reasons why.

***

Brad was fitted for a new brace at his doctor appointment with orders to start daily water therapy. His incisions were healed, and everything had stayed in position during the fall. The twinges were caused by the muscles reacting to the jolt and pressure of the fall. The doctor said that water therapy would loosen the muscles while building strength in them. He then suggested going through a horse therapy program after the water therapy. This would help align the hips with his spine. The motion of the horse's natural rhythm at a walk would open and stretch the hip flexors and stretch the tendons and muscles around the hips. It would also help strengthen his core and balance.

Brad was ready to do whatever it took to get out of the brace for good. His thoughts were to do his water therapy close to home to give Sarah some space. The last time he saw her at the B&B she didn't seem at ease around him. Up until the night of the storm he could feel the mutual attraction, but her past with Cole had more power over her, causing her to pull away.

He had let Travis know of his plans, and reassured him that all the remodeling was under control. The contractors were lined up to finish the first floor remodeling. Each room would be handicapped accessible, and he would stop in and approve their final work.

Chapter 25

Several weeks flew by before Jill had completed the clothes for the models. She worked hard before adding her 'Unique One' jewelry for them to wear. Everything was mailed out to the B&B, and she was set to fly back to Ohio by the end of the work week.

Travis had agreed with his Grandma, Greta and Sarah about not doing the books for the fundraiser's event. Sarah and her girls also agreed to be models and sent their sizes to Jill.

The winner of the competition was notified of all the details to see their selection of fabric on the doll of their choice. Jill had organized everything for Travis's live runway show. She couldn't wait to fly back home.

***

Sarah was excited to see Jill today and share her experiences she had at church. She and her girls had been attending church with Clara and Joe, so it was now part of their routine and they looked forward to Sunday mornings.

Jill drove to the B&B earlier than expected. She wanted to surprise Sarah and the girls.
Her nerves were getting to her as she hopped out of the car. The excitement of the fundraiser and anticipation of seeing Travis made her jittery and excited.

Sarah and the girls were in the kitchen putting blank tags on each lunch basket. The tags were for the contestants. Once they arrived, Tessa's assignment was to instruct them to fill out the tag with their name and list what they brought to put in the basket to auction.

"Surprise!" Jill exclaimed, and ran into the kitchen.

Sarah and the girls screamed for joy. They dropped what they were doing and ran toward her, embracing her in a group hug.

The girls were all talking at the same time. Jill giggled as they told her they were in love with the outfits she'd made, and they couldn't wait to wear them on the runway. Then she heard the voice that she'd been waiting to hear.

"Well, look who's here." Travis walked over to the group and gave Jill a hug. "How ya doing?"

"I'm great! I am so excited for this weekend. I can't wait to get things started." Jill released her hold, but kept her arms around Travis's waist, and looked up at him. "The question is—are you ready?"

He smiled at her and gave her a quick squeeze, then confessed, "Jill, I couldn't have gotten this far without you. Thank you. You have been an amazing helper with the behind-the-scenes ideas, and making the outfits for all the models. Oh, and organizing the contest winner to be our special guest. You're a natural party planner. Hey, maybe you should change your profession."

She was soaking up all his compliments before responding. "Or—I could just add it to my profession. I am a woman ya know, and we're known to be multi-taskers."

Shaking his head with a smirk on his face, he gave her a little push, scooting her away. "Okay, Okay, whatever. But seriously though, since you're here now, why don't we have the models practice their walk, and I'll grab my mom—she'll be the narrator."

They all agreed on the time to meet on the runway dressed in their outfits. Jill wanted plenty of time between the dress rehearsal and the real show, in case alterations were needed for the outfits.

***

Brad was feeling good about himself. He had put all his time into working out with stretch bands and free-weights, while staying dedicated to the water therapy classes. He was also approved by his doctor to drive again. His reflexes and coordination with his legs were close to normal. He had gained strength in them and was using a walker during therapy. It was his hips that were behind on recovery. They were tight and seemed to lock up. He thought it was a great idea to add the horse therapy to his regular therapy. He was up for anything and everything that would speed up the recovery time to be whole again.

Feeling a bit anxious, he drove toward Gunner's B&B, wondering if he would run into Sarah, and how she would react. His mission was to give the final inspection on the remodeling project and avoid running into her. Since he wasn't ready for any kind of snub or avoidance, his plan was to be in better physical shape before attempting any kind of relationship with her. And, even though he was in pretty good shape, he still had a lot of healing to do around the hip area. He really wanted to drive to the B&B just to talk to Bobby Sue about horse therapy.

*****

Jill blew her whistle to get everyone's attention. She giggled. "Wow, it worked. Okay, I know there needs to be some alterations on a few outfits, so—those who need them should come and stand by me. The rest of you stand by Travis. He will get you lined up in the order of the narrations."

"Oh, I can help with that, Travis." Laughter became louder as the appearance of the person speaking approached the runway.

Jill froze when she heard the voice—the voice she never wanted to hear again, or for that matter, the annoying laughter.

Sabrina walked up on the stage and gave Travis a bear hug. "Surprise!"

Travis eyes were wider than his smile. "Yeah—Yeah, this is a surprise. What—why are you here?"

Sabrina released her hug and explained, "I had some extra time on my hands so when you told me about your event I thought to myself, why not surprise him, and help run the runway show. Remember—I won the runway competition in New York? So who would be better to help out? Me, of course."

Jill felt like all eyes were aimed at her when her face became flushed. Something inside her surged, and she wanted to put her claim on Travis. Clearing her throat loudly, she put her clipboard down, and headed straight toward Travis. Greta made a quick forward motion and looped her arm into Jill's, and directed her to the opposite end of the porch. This was not the place to let emotions act out.

Speaking loudly, Greta asked, "I really need some alterations done on my outfit. Can mine be the first one you look at?"

Jill's expression was frozen. She glared at Greta, with all kinds of thoughts running out of her mouth. "Why is she here? It doesn't seem like he invited her. We don't need her. I hope he tells her to go back home."

Greta was just about to say something when Brad pulled up in his truck. "Jill! Look!"

Annoyed, Jill replied. "What?!"

Greta responded with a question. "What do you mean what? Just then she looked in the direction of Brad's truck. "Oh thank goodness—he's here! And—driving?"

Jill ran to him and opened his door and threw her arms around him. "Oh, Brad! I'm so glad you're here. And—look at you—you're driving!

Travis was thankful for his sister intervening between Jill and Sabrina's close encounter. Thinking quickly, he had to come up with a way to keep them apart this weekend. He pulled out his phone and texted his best friend, Jonah. Hopefully, he could help distract one of them during the event.

Ding, went his phone. It was from Jonah. "Hey, I got your text. Right now I'm working on my car, but if I can get it running I'll be over."

Travis ran his hand through his hair and blew out a long breath. He texted him back. "Okay man, hope to see you soon!"

150

Chapter 26

Jill could hardly focus on the alterations. Greta made sure she stayed behind the sewing machine and far away from Sabrina. She didn't know if Jill's aggressive reaction toward Sabrina was for her brother's attention, or because Sabrina won the competition in New York. Either way, Greta had some defusing work to do. She grabbed her Bible and sat on the opposite side of the room, beside the doorway. Looking through the highlighted verses that she had marked in her Bible was a quick way to find verses that spoke to her.

Jill was self-destructing, making Sabrina's appearance an attack on herself.

She turned the sewing machine off. "There! I'm done!" Anxious to know what Travis and Sabrina were doing, she suggested. "We should go and see what everyone is doing, and check that these alterations will work."

Greta placed her finger on the Scripture that she found to share with Jill. "Okay— we can do that. But I want to share a verse with you that will turn your frustration into the calmer, more collected Jill that I know."

Jill held the outfits in her hand, feeling embarrassed by the way she had reacted earlier.

Quietly, she agreed, "Okay."

"Let me paraphrase what Galatians 5:13 says. As Christians, we are free to choose to follow our sinful nature by devouring one another. But if we do, we will only be destroyed by each other. Instead, we are to serve one another in love."

Jill acknowledged her, and prayed a firm request. "Lord, please help me show love to Sabrina and set an example to Sarah and the girls. Don't let her push my buttons. And please send her running home as soon as possible. Amen."

Greta had a smirk on her face. "Okay. Well, I'm pretty sure you prayed from your heart with a few honest requests."

***

Sarah's excitement was shining on her face knowing Brad was back. Even though they never made eye contact, her eyes were attentive to his whereabouts. She couldn't wait to spend time with him. Too much time had passed by, and she had so much to tell him. The main thing she wanted to share was what she learned through a sermon called, 'Letting Go of What You Can't Control.' And she wanted to let him know that she wanted to spend more time getting to know him.

Their practice finished when Sarah saw Brad at the barn. She was all set to walk over and see him when Jill and Greta walked onto the porch.

Everyone turned their heads toward the parking lot when Jonah pulled in with his jalopy of a car. The car was so loud they could hardly hear Jill announce that she had completed the alterations. Then she asked Travis if they could all run through the formation again, so she and Greta would know what to do.

He agreed and watched Jonah get out of his car wearing a cowboy hat.

Jonah tipped his hat and greeted the group. "Howdy."

No one really responded as the tension in the air was thick, and all eyes were back on Jill and Sabrina.

Travis walked over to Jonah and shook his hand. "Hey, I'm glad you're here." Then he whispered, "But why are you wearing a cowboy hat and where did you get it? You're a computer whiz."

Jonah lifted the hat off his head and replied, "What, this old hat? Well, I remembered hearing Sabrina has a thing for guys wearing cowboy hats, so I thought I'd wear one. You know, to keep her distracted."

Travis shook his head and punched Jonah's arm. "Look. I need you to…." He directed his eyes toward Sabrina. He hoped Jonah would follow his eye movement and go stand with Sabrina.

Jonah looked at Travis with inquisitive eyes. He wasn't sure what he wanted him to do.

Jill walked toward Sabrina and extended her hand out to introduce herself.

Travis wasn't sure of Jill's intentions. Jonah just stood there watching. When she threw her hand out like a drill sergeant, Travis sprinted over to Jill, and lowered her arm. He kept his hand there. Then he laid his other arm around her shoulder. Immediately, Jill's body language softened.

Travis cleared his throat. "Um, Jill this is Sabrina. She's the daughter of the CEO who runs the largest convention in the doll industries. She and her Dad have taken me under their wing to help me get started with my doll line.

Sabrina was all smiles and moved in closer to wrap her arm around his upper arm. "Yes—we've been business partners for over a year now and have become more than that lately. We've become…"

Travis released himself from Sabrina's hold and sent a panicked look at Jonah. This was too close for comfort. Jonah tossed his hands up, not knowing what to do. Travis then turned toward Jill, blocking her view of Sabrina. "Listen, we have to finish up here or we won't get everything done before show time."

Jill's body went stiff. The only things that moved were her eyes. And they were looking straight up at him. "Travis! Aren't you going to tell Sabrina who I am, and how long we've known each other?"

The room went still. Jill could hear her heart pounding in her ears and beads of sweat were forming on Travis's forehead. Time stood still. Travis's thoughts flashed back to when he and Jill first met. It was at the college Bible study group that had met every Wednesday night at his parent's house. She'd joined, the group four years ago. They had an immediate connection. She was able to release any tension that he had by her cute little sayings. Her 'fun sized' personality was what he adored the most about her. They'd shared a lot of first time events together. He could still hear the excitement in her voice as she landed her first fish in the boat without a net. And he loved teaching her how to shoot targets with his 380 pistol. She thought it would be a cute idea to shoot a happy face into the target paper. During the summer Jill would jump on the back of his Honda CBR 1000 and they would go exploring.

Jill tugged at his arm, while holding a conversation with him through her stare. Communicating the love they'd once had. Finally, she got his attention. "Travis!"

Travis swallowed hard. Then he rubbed her arms. The passion that he once had for her filled his heart. They did have a love connection. They were heading toward getting engaged, once she graduated. But then his emotions changed when he let himself continue to think. Back to when she chose her career over him the night of her graduation party.

"Sabrina, this is Jill. She is the one who has been my right hand in organizing this fund raiser. I owe it to her to let her continue with her ideas and to run the show. But I do appreciate your thoughtfulness in wanting to help."

Jill seemed pleased that he made it clear she was in charge. She dropped her concern that he had not told Sabrina she had been his girlfriend for two years. So, Sabrina had no business to stay any longer and was free to go home.

Sabrina faked a smile before responding. "No problem, Cowboy. Where would you like me to help out?"

Greta saw the look on Jill's face when she heard Sabrina call him Cowboy. It was like a foul odor blew in. "Hey, I say we finish up with this practice so I can work with the new horse."

Being grateful for his sister's suggestion, Travis agreed. Then he excused himself from Sabrina. He took Jill's hand and led her to her spot in the lineup.

Jonah placed the cowboy hat back on his head and walked over to Sabrina. He was glad she still referred to Travis as being a cowboy. It proved his case with Travis as to why he had to wear a cowboy hat. "Hey, remember me?"

Sabrina looked at him, then at his hat, and back at him. "Sure. You're Travis's friend who picked us up from the airport one time."

Jonah smiled, "Yeah, that was me. Hey, would you mind helping me with something?"

Sabrina glanced over toward Travis and saw he was busy talking among everyone. Then she let out a long sigh. "Yeah, sure— what is it you need help with?"

Jonah stuttered a little, trying to think of something he could occupy her with. A computer engineer is one of many things he excelled at, so he thought of showing her the ad campaign for the dolls. She seemed interested, so they went to Travis's office. Once Jonah pulled up the ads on the computer screen, they were in a deep conversation over all the details.

Chapter 27

Brad approved the construction work for the handicapped rooms. Next on his agenda? Talking with Bobby Sue about a horse therapy program. He watched the rehearsal from his room at the barn, thinking it would be best to wait for her there. It was Sarah's turn. He opened the window so he could hear Bobby Sue's speech.

"The next group of dolls will represent our rodeo dolls."

Greta, Jake and Sarah walked on stage. Sarah walked forward, and Bobby Sue continued.

"The first one is our Gymkhana doll. Her name is Sarah. She is sporting leather chaps, with a cropped-style vest layered over a western yoke, button-up shirt. The leather belt with a championship belt buckle is one of many she has won in the barrel racing division. Boot-cut jeans tucked into her boots with a tan color cowboy hat completes her outfit. Her 'Unique One' accessory is the removable beaded band on her cowboy hat. It can be worn as a necklace also."

Sarah removed her hat and unclipped the beaded-band. Then she hung it from her fingers to show the potential audience. She twirled her hat and tossed it up in the air. Her head dipped in a smooth swooping motion to place the hat back on her head.

Bobby Sue continued. "Thank you Sarah. The next rodeo doll represents a...."

She described Jake as the bull rider doll and Greta as the drill team rider doll.

***

Brad closed the window and caught himself smiling. Sarah looked sexy and confident twirling her hat, then catching it with her head. She did it as one complete move. It made him wonder if it was her signature move—from her past.

Bobby Sue met Brad after the rehearsal, while everyone else scrambled to get things set up. Their conversation was brief because there was so much to do before the public would arrive.

"Brad, I would love to have a therapeutic program here. As a matter of fact, it's been on my mind ever since I talked with a gal at the last event where we performed. You know, where I found our new horse?"

Brad grinned and became hopeful. "Yeah...."

She rambled on, "Her name was Cheyanne and she has a therapeutic program out in Wyoming, I think—yeah, that's where she's from. Anyway, I could get in touch with her now that I have a reason to act on my good intentions. Maybe she can tell me the ins and outs of the business."

He reached over and hugged her. "That sounds great to me. Can you let me know if you talk with her?"

Bobby Sue returned his hug. "Absolutely! I'll get right on it after this fund raiser. Speaking of which, I should get back over there to see what I can do to help out. You'll be here tomorrow, right? We have lots of lunch baskets to bid on."

Brad laughed. "Yes, I'm looking forward to a surprise lunch."

***

It was an hour before the sun would set. Jill asked Sarah if she could help arrange the Unique One jewelry, on her merchant table. She agreed, as she wanted to talk to her about Brad.

They heard Jonah's car leaving as Sabrina and Travis walked by. He was carrying boxes to a table two down from Jill's. They were in a deep conversation about the accessories he ordered for the dolls. The table between them was for Grandpa Joe. He would display his custom made doll houses, available for bidding during the silent auction. They stood and watched Travis carry three boxes, while Sabrina played with her hair.

In a disgusted voice, Jill said, "Would you look at that! Is she such a diva that she can't even carry a box?"

Sarah looked over her shoulder at them and smirked. "Maybe he's trying to impress her."

Jill snapped a look at her and huffed at the thought of it. "There is something about that girl that I just don't like."

"Yeah, I know what you mean." Sarah thought back to a time when Cole and a few of his bull riding buddies were setting up a merchant table for a rodeo. She was warming up her horse in the arena when she heard Rosa and a few other girls giggling and talking to the bull riders. Rosa and her friends purchased tee-shirts and put them on, so the riders could sign them.

Sarah sighed, "There's something about flirtatious girls that guys seem to go weak in the knees over." She kept on working, but with a conscious eye on the barn door. She didn't want to miss the chance to talk with Brad.

Brad had had his driving restriction lifted, allowing him to drive to and from work, doctor's appointments, and family emergencies. He was not allowed to drive after sunset. And it was getting close to that time. He was pushing his curfew, so he headed for his truck.

Sarah smiled when she saw Brad by his truck. She hoped he was moving back now that he was able to drive himself. Wanting to know more, she questioned Jill. "When you talked with Brad earlier, did he say when he'd be back to work?"

Jill took a moment to think of what their conversation was about. "Actually, I didn't even ask him. I was too upset with Sabrina showing up. But, he did tell me that he was here to talk with Bobby Sue about horse therapy."

Sarah looked puzzled. "Horse therapy? For himself?"

Jill replied, "Yes, he has been doing water therapy, and the doctor says that horse therapy will stretch and strengthen the muscles and tendons around the hip area. I guess they are tight. So he was going to ask Bobby Sue if he could do it here."

Sarah nodded her head. "Sounds interesting. I hope he can." Not taking her eyes off him, she ran her fingers through her hair and tucked her shirt in. She watched him get in his truck and hoped he would drive over to talk with her. He looked over and caught her eye. She smiled and gave him a small wave with her hand. She could see his smile as he waved and drove away.

Book club questions for discussion.   Chapters 22-27

❖ *In Chapter 22 Sarah has a revelation when she lets nature speak to her during her soul walk. Have you experienced a time where nature spoke to you in a surprising way? If not, take time to be still and allow God to speak to you through His Creation. It will draw you closer to the Creator of the Universe.*

❖ *In Chapter 23, Sarah described the church's atmosphere. A lot of churches have changed with the times over the years. Do you think they are more inviting/appealing to people to simply 'come as they are' than in years past? Why or why not? What are the pros and cons of the changes?*

❖ *Read Romans 12 and share what verses empowers you the most and why?*

❖ *Romans 10: 8, 9, 10 teaches us how to become Christians. Some people think it must be a complicated process, but it is not. What other verses in the Bible explain how to receive salvation?*

❖ *Greta shares in Chapter 26 that she uses a highlighter in her Bible to mark the verses that speak to her. Is this something you do as well to quickly find scriptures that speak to you?*

❖ *When Greta reminded Jill of what Galatians 5:13 says, Jill began to pray for a changed heart toward Sabrina. Have you been in a position where someone has pushed your buttons and you reacted wrongly?*

Book club questions for discussion.   *Chapters 22-27*

❖ *Did you try to retract your actions afterwards? Were you able to do it on your own or with the help of prayer?*

❖ *Don't you just love those "Sabrina" gals? They truly test our character about how we should perceive them and our own mannerisms. What are some ways we can befriend them without stirring up our own emotions?*

Chapter 28

The girls were the first to wake. They looked forward to being doll models on stage, wearing their new outfits. But they were mostly excited about the live gold fish game. They lay in bed thinking of names to call their gold fish when they won them.

"Mommy, wake up. Today is the day for the big party!" Tessa said, shaking her shoulder.

Sarah moaned. "What time is it?" She could not fall asleep the night before. Negative thoughts kept filling her head about why Brad hadn't made any attempt to talk to her the day before. It had been weeks since they last talked.

Tessa told her the time, and then asked if they could go on down to the kitchen to eat with Clara and Joe. Sarah sat up in bed and gave them all a hug.

"Yes, you can. I'll be down shortly." She flipped off her covers and stretched before going over to the window. As she looked out the window she saw the guys were setting up the kids' games and roping off areas that were not part of the event. Her excitement about the day had faded when Brad had waved and driven away last night without stopping to talk to her.

***

Clara and Bobby Sue were arranging the lunch baskets as they were being dropped off at the auction table. Jack and Jake hung the last speaker and tested all the microphones while car after car kept coming in. Sarah kept her eye out for Brad's truck. No sign of him.

She thought to herself. *Is he coming? Surely he would—he wouldn't miss this big event—would he? Is he avoiding me? And why? Oh come on Brad, pull in!*

She walked over to the quilt table and stared at the full-size wedding quilt that was up for raffle. Gently rubbing her hand across the hand quilted top made her feel sad. She missed being married. She missed being loved by her husband, and she missed Brad.

One of the quilting ladies touched her shoulder and whispered. "Excuse me, but we are asking people not to touch the quilts."

Sarah apologized, then pulled out some money to buy a raffle ticket.

***

Behind the stage, the girls eagerly waited to walk the runway. Bobby Sue had finished the welcome speech when Sarah peaked through the curtains to look for Brad one more time. The modeling show was about to start and Jill was the first one up.

"Jill is our career doll—a college graduate with a degree in hand. Sharp minded. Future focused. With a loving, gentle heart. Eager to make a positive mark in the business world."

Bobby Sue paused, and stood. Then she walked to the front of the stage with a career doll in hand.

Holding her smile, Jill's mind got to work. *Okay, what is she doing? The script says to ask for applause and then I'm to walk off stage.*

"You see, this career doll—Jill—carries Jesus in her heart. She will walk wherever He guides her." Bobby Sue lifted the doll to the audience and pointed to the marking on the right foot. "Etched on the bottom of her foot is a symbol of His love, as a reminder to walk His path and not the world's."

The audiences seemed as surprised as Jill was by the etched marking. She tried to hold back her tears. This was not scripted by her. The etched marking on the doll's foot was news to her. It was like a direct message to her heart, from Travis. *Did Travis add this as a way of showing his acceptance to my feelings about our future? Has he closed the door for us—permanently?*

Bobby Sue walked back to her chair. "Thank you Jill. How about a round of applause for our career doll?"

Jill waved as she left the stage. She wanted to find Travis and ask what provoked the surprise etching on her doll.

Bobby Sue added a plug for her Unique One jewelry line. "Jill has a merchant table set up under the canopy. All the models' accessories are handmade by Jill. You can meet her and have a chance to buy any life-sized or matching doll size accessories after the show. Okay, next we have…"

It was Sarah's turn on the runway. As Bobby Sue introduced her, Sarah scanned the audience looking for Brad. Standing at the front of the stage, she didn't see him. Then she did her famous move from her past—twirling her hat in the air and having it land on her head. The audience hooped and hollered. She took a cowgirl curtsy, and when she lifted her eyes back up she saw him. Brad was standing up applauding.

The local TV station met Jill at her merchant table. They wanted to hear more about her jewelry line. Jill was excited to talk to the reporters, and to have her jewelry line viewed on TV. But her main thoughts were on Travis.

The applause from the stage caught the TV reporter's attention. Jill stopped talking as they all looked toward the stage. There he was. Travis and all the little girls. Tessa was wearing a yellow daisy sun dress with white tennis shoes and a Unique One daisy necklace. Elise was sporting a romper with an open toe sandal and a navy blue eyelet ball cap on her head. She had navy blue leather cuff bands wrapped around her pony tails, custom made by Jill to match her ball cap.

Travis held Aubrey's and Kendra's hands as they walked to the front of the stage. Jill took a deep breath and smiled as she exhaled. She was so happy for him. This was the end of their chapter and a new beginning for their careers. She felt an unknowing peace about it. This was really the time to let go.

Bobby Sue was most excited about the last set of dolls to walk the runway—her parents. "Coming soon will be two more dolls, featured as—Grandparents!

Every family desires loving grandparents. They love to tell stories of 'when they were young.' These tales are fun to pass down as stories or traditions. Clara and Joe, will you come forward?"

Everyone applauded as they entered the stage.

"Grandma Clara is wearing an apron printed with chicken and hens, crafted by herself. She likes to tease people by telling them she runs the roost—with her husband's approval."

The crowd laughed.

"Grandpa Joe is a 'jack of all trades' doll. He is wearing carpenter pants. He says there's never enough pockets when working in carpentry. He makes doll houses and doll furniture. And he has them at a table for sale under the canopy. Stop by and see his custom doll houses exclusively designed for the 'U-Can-Be' dolls.

"There's a book in the Bible called Titus. Chapters two and three talk about our responsibilities, as grandparents or the older generation.

"Clara and Joe strive to live by those examples. She teaches younger women to love their husbands and children, to be self-controlled and pure. To be busy at home and kind to all.

"In everything, Joe tries to set an example by doing good, showing self-control, integrity, seriousness and sound speech that cannot be condemned."

"Before we end, I would like to thank each one of you who came to support our Bed and Breakfast fundraiser. We are very excited to open again soon and meet people from all parts of the world and different walks of life.

"In about thirty minutes we will auction off the lunch baskets right here. So mingle and if you don't know someone, introduce yourselves. We don't want you to go away as a stranger. There are lots of silent bids going on at the different tables. A lot of the local businesses have donated things to be auctioned off. The local quilt club has also donated a variety of table runners and wall quilts. There is a beautiful hand-made wedding quilt being raffled off at 5:00 today. Thank you. And again, we will be back in thirty minutes for the lunch basket auction."

Chapter 29

Determined to talk to Brad today, Sarah made her way through the crowd before he could disappear. She couldn't wait to tell him that she was in a new place—in her head. She had learned to let go of what she couldn't control. Not being able to let go of the past was where she was when Brad embraced her on the porch. Rejection was where she had left him. But now she was open to new beginnings, ready to explore her options. She wanted to see if she could win his friendship back, then see where it could go from there.

Standing with his back toward her, she thought she would surprise him by putting her hands over his eyes and make him guess who it was. She was only two rows away when she saw a girl hurrying by, calling out his name.

"Brad?"

He was standing at the side of the aisle waiting for the crowd to thin out when he heard his name. He looked around to see who it was.

"Oh, I can't believe it's you! You're walking!"

Brad's eyes caught up to the voice. "Tara? Wow. I didn't expect to see you here. I thought you were living in New York."

She ran up and hugged him.

As he embraced her, he noticed Sarah was standing there, just a few feet away. Their eyes met. Then she quickly turned and walked off.

Tara replied, "I do live in New York but I wanted to surprise Jill and support the event."

He let go of Tara and tried to see where Sarah was heading.

She continued to babble. "Enough about me. Look at you. How long have you been walking? How ya feeling? You look great!"

He chuckled, "Oh Tara, It's great to see you and hear your forever questioning self. Do you want to grab a seat?

"Yeah sure."

***

There was a crowd at Travis's merchant table. People were buying his dolls and having the live models sign them. Sabrina and Jonah were in charge, checking items at the cash register and restocking the tables.

Jill looked radiant sitting on a stool at her podium. This was her request. As short as she was, she didn't want to be too overwhelmed with people all around her. It also gave her the opportunity to watch her Unique One jewelry table. Bobby Sue and Bo offered to be at her table and work the sales for her.

Joe's voice came over the PA system loud and clear. "Okay, folks. Can I have your attention? Bring your appetite and your loaded pockets over to the stage area. It's time for the lunch box auction. The merchant tables will reopen after the final bid.

Sarah stood behind the table with her three girls. They were teasing each other about who would be their lunch date. After Sarah saw Brad hugging a random girl, she wished she hadn't entered one.

Each participant stood behind her own lunch baskets. In front of each baskets was a label describing who made it and what was in the basket. The rules stipulated that the highest bidder should claim his lunch and enjoy a one-hour lunch with the person who made it.

Clara took over on the microphone. Picking up the card in front of the first basket, she began, "Okay, first up we have…"

Travis, Brad and Jonah were standing next to each other as the auction started.

Brad looked at Travis and Jonah. "Hey guys, I'm in a pinch. You see, I really want to bid on Sarah's and the girls' lunch baskets. But by surprise, Tara is here. I really treated her badly before she left for New York and I should bid on hers."

Travis nodded his head. "Yeah, I'm sort of in the same boat. I have Jill and Sabrina wanting me to bid on their baskets."

Jonah stood between them, cool as a cucumber. "What happens if you buy them both?"

Travis glared at him, then jabbed him in the ribs. "They would eat me for lunch! Wait. You can outbid me on Sabrina's basket."

"Why would I do that? She doesn't want to eat with me. She wants you."

Travis sighed, "I know, but I can't do that to Jill. This has been our production project, our local town. I have to buy her basket."

Clara's voice caught their attention. "Next up, we have three young girls who have been working in the kitchen since they moved here. In my opinion, they're fine lunch makers." The crowd laughed.

"Listen up folks. This is a three-for-one deal. The first basket was made by Tessa. She made a one and a half inch thick peanut butter and jelly sandwich. We have a tape measure up here to prove it."

The crowd laughed again. But not Brad. His eyes kept roaming back and forth from Sarah to Tara. Sarah kept her eyes down. She didn't want to engage with the crowd at all. She wanted to hide in the kitchen until this whole thing was over.

Clara continued, "The second basket was made by her sister, Elise. She has all the side snacks you would want on a picnic. A bag of carrot sticks, corn chips, and grapes."

Travis looked at Jonah. "Okay, you understand the plan—right?"

Jonah stood there longer than Travis liked. "Right? You are to outbid me every time, to make it look like I am trying for Sabrina's...."

Brad interrupted, "Hey, maybe you could do that for me?"

Jonah backed up a bit waving his hands. "Wait, I can't eat two lunch baskets."

"Sorry, Brad, but I need him more than you. You'll have to figure your problem out on your own." Travis insisted.

Brad sighed as he listened to the final detail of Aubrey's basket.

"Aubrey has cupcakes in her basket…" Then, as Aubrey interrupted her, Clara responded. "What did you say, honey?"

Aubrey said, a little bit louder, that her cupcakes have sprinkles on them.

Brad smiled. He really missed spending time with Sarah's girls. He looked over to Sarah, willing her to look at him. Discouragement came over him. He thought, *Maybe she is still not open to spending time with me. I shouldn't make her uncomfortable, so I'll go ahead and buy Tara's basket.*

"Okay folks, you heard it. What will it be? Can I get a starting bid?"

The bidding started off low for the girls.

Brad lifted his hand. "I bid twenty-five dollars each for the three baskets, totaling seventy-five dollars."

"Going once—going twice—sold! Brad, will you meet your lunch dates at the stairs?"

He walked forward so Clara could hear him. "Before I take my winning lunch baskets I would like to bid on one more."

Clara looked over at Joe. "Can he do that?"

Joe nodded his head and replied. "The boy must have deep pockets. And that's what we like at a fund raiser. Let him keep bidding."

Everyone laughed. Tara's eyes brightened when she heard he wanted to bid on one more basket. Sarah was touched that he bought her girls' baskets and was sure he wouldn't be buying hers.

"Well, let's not keep this man waiting. Which lunch box do you want to bid on?"

Brad was still open to buying Sarah's basket. All she had to do is show him a sign. Any sign letting him know that she wanted him to buy hers.

Sarah's throat went dry. She could feel her heart beating faster. People in the crowd were yelling their advice on which one to pick.

"I would like to bid on Tara's." Brad said. She smiled as she bounced up and down, clapping her hands. Then he quickly glanced at Sarah.

Sarah looked over at Tara and then back at her own basket. She rubbed her hand over the top of her basket. Tara's excitement brought back memories of how she felt when Cole bought her lunch basket long ago. *Maybe you only get one shot at love….*

"Sold! To Brad for forty-five dollars. Thank you, Brad. Now, go and collect your gals and enjoy your lunches."

Brad felt pretty special. He could see how happy the three girls were that he bought their lunch baskets. Tara was excited as well. But in the pit of his stomach he had an ache. He wanted Sarah.

Sitting close to the stage at a picnic table, they were able to watch the rest of the auction. The girls wanted to see who would buy their mommy's basket. Brad scanned the crowd wondering what guy would get to spend a one-on-one with her. He slowly swallowed the peanut butter and jelly sandwich when he heard she was up next. He excused himself. He stated that he wanted to buy a bottle of water, and asked the girls if they wanted one too. They all said yes. He rushed as fast as he could to the drink table where Jake was stationed to work. He could hear the bids climbing as he got closer to the table.

Finally, he was able to ask Jake to bid on Sarah's basket. Pulling money out from his pockets he asked him to outbid the highest bidder and buy her basket—for himself.

Jake was confused as to why he wanted him to do it. "You already have four baskets. How many more do you want?"

"Hurry! Don't ask questions. Just do it for me, please! I'll wait here until you can come back. Go on! Go!"

Jake took the money and ran up to the front of the stage. "I bid…" looking down at the folded money that Brad gave him, he counted one hundred dollars. He continued, "I bid one hundred dollars!"

Sarah's eyes got big as the crowd whooped and hollered. This was the highest bid so far.

Down came the gavel. "Sold! To the highest bidder of the day!"

Sarah met Jake at the steps—and thanked him for buying her basket. He nodded his head and then asked if she could wait until after the last basket was sold to have their lunch date. He explained that he had to get back to the drink table just until the auction was over. She understood and agreed. Then she watched him head back to the table and saw Brad was standing there.

"Next up is my granddaughter, Greta. In her basket we have a peanut butter and banana sandwich on wheat bread, cheddar chips and black licorice. That sounds like a custom made lunch basket. Let's see who the lucky guy will be. Can I get twenty-five, twenty-five dollars…"

Joe yelled out, "We have twenty-five."

Greta looked to see who it was but didn't see anyone raise their hand. Apparently her grandpa did.

Clara continued on, "Okay, can I have thirty? Thirty-five?"

Clara saw a hand go up. Then she asked for forty. Again Joe yelled out. "We have forty."

Greta looked around to see whose hand went up. She only saw the guy who had her basket at thirty-five. Clara was confused also. She looked at her husband to confirm with him that she saw a new bidder. Joe smiled at her and nodded.

Clara continued with the bidding. "Okay folks, can I have fifty? Fifty seems to be the number today. Anyone? Fifty? Okay! Sold to the mystery person for forty dollars."

Greta had hoped Jack would have bid on her basket. They were all the things he liked. It was what he packed when he helped her mend the fencing around the property. But she didn't see him in the crowd. She picked up her basket and headed to the stage steps while wondering who would meet her there. And there he was—Jack in his ball cap.

Greta's smile was big. "So, did you bid on my basket?"

Jack nodded, "Uh, yep. I couldn't resist the black licorice."

She laughed. "But where were you standing? Oh, wait. You were the one grandpa claimed the bid for. Did you have this pre-planned?"

He grabbed the handle of the basket and smiled. "You could say that." Then they walked off.

Clara continued with the auction. "Okay, folks. We save the finest two baskets for last."

Sabrina, here on my right, comes all the way from Tennessee. She shopped at our local deli. In her basket is an Everything bagel with cream cheese, a side salad, and macadamia cookies. To my left belongs to our top model, Jill, our career doll. She has in her basket a croissant sandwich with tomato, turkey, cheese and mayo, bread and butter pickle wedges and iced brownies. Now since these are the last two baskets, I'm going to let the bidder call out the name of which basket they want. Who wants to open the bid?"

Sabrina and Jill's eyes were locked on Travis.

The bids were going back and forth on the girls' basket. Slowly the bidders dropped off.

Clara noticed her grandson had not offered a bid. "Do we have any new bidders out there who haven't bid yet? It's for a good cause.

Come on, the last bid called was forty-five dollars. Do I have any more bidders out there?"

Travis raised the bid to fifty dollars for each basket. The girls smiled. Then they gave a quick look at each other then back to Travis. He elbowed Jonah.

Jonah glanced at him then called out, "I raise the bid two dollars for Sabrina's basket."

The crowd laughed. Sabrina's face dropped. She stared at Travis, willing him to raise his bid. The pressure was on Travis. She began to pout, giving him her famous puppy dog eyes. Rubbing the back of his neck, he looked at Jill, then back at Sabrina. But before he could get a word out, Clara dropped the gavel to the table and said, "Sold! Thank you folks for coming out...."

Sabrina huffed and squinted her eyes while glaring at Travis. As she walked off stage carrying her basket to Jonah, she threw a dirty look at Jill.

Chapter 30

As they sat down, Sarah thanked Jake again for bidding on her lunch basket as they sat down. He reassured her that it was his pleasure to buy it. After all, he was buying it with someone else's money, and he got to eat the winnings. They sat quietly as they ate their lunch. Jake wasn't much of a talker. And he wasn't sure why Brad asked him to buy her lunch basket. Looking around he saw his brother, Jack, laughing with Greta. So, to end the quietness, he asked Sarah if she would like to join them.

Not wanting to be near Brad, she looked to see where he was sitting. She couldn't wrap her head around how the day had played out. Sarah had fully planned to talk with Brad and tell him she was ready to start over with their friendship. With her renewed mind about her life, she wanted to begin it with him. But seeing him hug another girl and then buying her basket, was a clear sign to her that he had moved on from thinking about her.

Jake cleared his throat, "I mean—we don't have to if you don't want to. I thought maybe you would be more comfortable sitting with Greta since you and I don't really know each other."

Sarah smiled. "I'm sorry. I was distracted with my thoughts. Well, okay. May I ask you why you bought my basket?"

Jack squirmed. He was sitting in the hot seat now. Not knowing what he should say, he blurted out, "Because I like Wickles pickles."

He looked at her and she stared back at him. Then they both began to laugh so hard it drew the attention of Brad and Tara.

The girls had run off to play the games, which had been their main agenda for today. They were each bound to win a gold fish. Tara watched Brad's expression as he watched Jake and Sarah laughing so wholeheartedly. He had no idea that it was a simple stress release for

Sarah to laugh fully. So, it gave him a false reading on how she was enjoying her time with Jake.

I made a big mistake asking him to buy her lunch, he thought. They look like they are connecting with each other. And to top it off, I paid for him to spend time with her.

Tara spoke first. "Who is that over there?"

Brad replied without taking his eyes off them. "That's Jake. He lives and works here. He's Jack's twin brother. And that's Sarah. She's the mom to the three girls that we had lunch with."

Tara nodded and then remembered. "Oh, yeah. Sarah and her three girls are the ones Jill met in New York last year. Okay. And now they are living here, right?"

Brad nodded when he looked at Tara and smiled. "Tara, I've been wanting to talk with you about how I treated you before you left for New York."

Tara swallowed hard and stared at him. She wasn't sure what he was about to say. She thought she had let go of her feelings for him when she moved to New York. But, seeing him now…after he had just bought her lunch…brought back all those giddy feelings again.

He continued, "Um–yeah. I feel really bad about how I led you to believe that we were…you know…a couple."

He studied her face as it changed to a sad expression. He could see that he was hurting her all over again, only this time he could feel it, too. She blinked a few times, trying to avoid flowing tears. Even knowing where their relationship was at this point in their lives still stung. The rejection of a past dream still pulled at the heart strings. Time stood still. Memories were going through her head as they came rushing back.

All she could say was what was the truth. "Yeah, it hurt."

Brad looked away. Then he looked back at Sarah. He knew where his heart wanted to be. He had to apologize for his wrongdoings if he wanted the Lord to bless him with a relationship with Sarah. He closed his eyes for a few seconds in an attempt to block out all the distractions. He prayed for the right words to come out of his heart and mouth—to please Him.

Then he looked at Tara and grabbed her hands before he could speak. His nerves were getting to him. He began to rub the tops of her hands with his thumbs.

"Tara, I want to start off by telling you that I did like you and I did enjoy spending time with you and still do…" He paused and looked her in the eyes. "But not like a girlfriend. I value our friendship to be more than that. Like a forever friend with whom I can just be myself, one where we laugh and talk. I feel that as a friend you will always have my back, and I will always have yours. But my heart…." He looked down at their hands as she pulled her hands away. She was breathing harder and he knew he had to finish with his apology and stay true to his words.

Continuing, he kept his stare low to avoid seeing the hurt in her eyes. "During the time we were rehearsing for the play, my emotions were controlling my actions. I enjoyed knowing and feeling your excitement when we were together. I ate it up. But I was really wanting those feelings from someone else. It would get me through the times of knowing I would never receive them from the other girl. So I allowed you to think we were a couple without saying we were." He looked at her. "Does that make any sense to you?"

She glanced away from his stare. "It was Jill that you wanted, right?"

He swallowed hard. "Yeah, at the time I thought she was the one for me. But not anymore." He glanced at Sarah and watched her smile at Jake. He wondered if he had lost her, too. Then he touched Tara's arm, causing her to look at him. "Hey. I would be crushed if I were to lose your friendship now, but I would understand if you don't want to be friends."

Tara wanted to end this conversation. It was too much for her. "Let's just leave the past in the past. It seems we've grown from our mistakes. And yes, we can continue being friends."

He was relieved that she accepted his apology and wanted to move on. He reached over and hugged her.

Tara hugged him back and whispered. "Don't get all crushing on me now. I just got over you."

He laughed. Then he let go of her. "I'm going to miss you."

She smiled. "I'm going to miss you, too. Maybe you can come see me in a play sometime whenever you come to New York?"

He smiled nodding his head. "I would love to!" Then he gave her one more hug before they stood and cleaned up their lunch. Looking over at Sarah, he saw her looking at him when he let go of Tara. She quickly looked away.

Chapter 31

Travis saw Greta and Jack eating lunch with Grandpa Joe at his merchant table. He thought it would be a safe zone to eat lunch there, too.

He took Jill by the hand and stated. "Let's join Greta and Jack for lunch."

Jill looked over where they were, and agreed. At some point she wanted to talk with him in private, but for now she wanted to enjoy the moment. In the distance ahead of them, she saw Sabrina and Jonah heading toward Grandpa Joe's table, too. And a huff stirred inside her.

"Are they joining us also?" She pointed toward Sabrina and Jonah.

He sighed. "It looks that way. Hey, I'm really sorry that she's here. I did not invite her."

Jill put her arm around his. Making her statement clear, she added, "I know. I actually know what her kind is. Don't worry, I won't lose my cool in front of your grandpa."

He felt relieved that he chose to eat at his grandpa's table. He thought, *If I can get through this luncheon in one piece, I could stay busy at my table talking with the people, and avoid both the girls until it's over.*

Greta and Jack were in a conversation with Grandpa Joe when they walked up to the table. Travis went to grab a chair for Jill when Sabrina and Jonah arrived at the table.

Sabrina hurriedly walked toward Travis and held onto the chair that he was about to grab. "What was wrong with my lunch basket? I thought you liked everything about me. That's why I put an Everything bagel in my basket."

Travis chuckled nervously, and glanced to see where Jonah was. "Well, apparently Jonah likes them too." Are you joining us for lunch? Let me grab another chair for you."

He grabbed another chair and carried them back to the table. He set one on each side of Grandpa Joe. The girls took their seats. And Travis stood centered between each of them.

Grandpa Joe kept a conversation going while Travis and Jonah scarfed down their lunches. Then Sabrina asked Travis if she could talk with him. He looked at Jill, who nodded in a way of excusing him to do so.

She frowned and gestured for him to go.

Walking away from the table Sabrina grabbed Travis's arm and asked him, "So—what's going on?"

He stopped far enough away from the table so that Jill couldn't hear him before he answered, "I'm thinking you should go."

Sabrina's eyebrows went up as she stared at him. "What?"

Travis squinted and he apologized. "I'm sorry. It's just...with Jill here—and everything going on, with trying to make sure you're comfortable, it's just too much for me. I don't think you're enjoying your time here either."

She was blown away with his honesty. But she took it well. She liked that he was concerned for her and her happiness. And he was right. She wasn't having a good time.

"Hmm...Well you're right. I think it's time I should go. But first, I'll need to check and see if there are any open seats available to Tennessee. If so, do you think your friend, Jonah, could give me a ride to the airport— in your jeep?"

He smiled, then laughed. "You remembered his jalopy. Yeah, he can use my jeep."

She leaned in and kissed his lips softly. Then they walked back to the table.

***

Travis said good bye to Sabrina and thanked Jonah for taking her to the airport. The night festivities were about to start. The band had arrived, and the music was playing loudly. Tara, Jill and Greta were line dancing, while Jack, Jake, Travis and Brad were boxing up the merchandise. The sale was over, and everyone was making their way to the dance floor for the evening. Sarah and the girls were helping Bobby Sue and Clara carry the last of the jellies and jams to the kitchen.

Sarah's phone rang. Questioning who it might be, she looked to see the number was from New York. She excused herself to the hallway before answering the call. It was the call she didn't want to get. The nursing home was letting her know her aunt had passed away in her sleep. She slumped down the wall onto the floor and wept.

The moon was bright, and the party was in full motion. Sarah collected herself enough to ask Clara to keep an eye on the girls. She told her about her aunt and explained that she wanted some time alone. Clara hugged her and told her she was sorry to hear about her loss and to take all the time she needed. And of course, she would be glad to take care of the girls.

Sarah slipped out the back porch and ran to the first corral. Grabbing a halter and a lead rope off the gate, she opened it and caught the first horse that came up to her. It was the new horse. She met the horse head on. He nickered. As she stood there staring, tears flowed from her eyes, blurring her vision. Blinking, she shook her head in disbelief of what was reality and what wasn't. She was trying to run from it all.

With shaking hands, she put the halter on him. She slowly lifted his forelock and touched the heart-shape marking embedded in his hair.

She whispered, "It's true. Traeh. It's you." The heart-shape marking confirmed the horse was Cole's. She remembered back when Cole explained to the girls why he named him Traeh. It was 'heart' spelled backwards. Traeh had a big heart.

"I knew in my heart when I first saw you from a distance that God brought you to me. You're the only one who understands my brokenness."

Jill and Greta were singing karaoke songs. The guys sat in the front row watching them make fools of themselves. Brad was concerned about Sarah's whereabouts. He saw Clara and the girls; but where was Sarah? He got up and moseyed around. He even went to the front porch thinking she might be on the porch swing. Out of the corner of his eye he saw a silhouette of a horse running out of the corral. Once it passed the light post he could see Sarah on its back as they galloped by him

He shouted, "Sarah!"

The horse made a mad dash for the open field as they rode as one past Brad. He was in disbelief. He spun around to see them fade into the darkness.

Sarah was crying out, "Why? Why do You have to take all the good people away from me? First you took Cole. Then Brad. And now my aunt. Why?" Her heart was pounding with the rhythm of the horse's hooves beating the ground.

Memories came flooding back—back to when it was her, Cole and his horse, Traeh. And when they first got him. Galloping aimlessly…hearing the horse huff and puff…feeling the wind blowing through her hair…seeing Cole riding beside her. She reached out to touch him when the horse came to an abrupt stop. Was it his image or her imagination? She fell forward and hugged the horse's neck as she lay there sobbing. The horse stood quietly in front of the fence row.

The clouds were moving in, covering the moonlit sky. It fit her mood. The darkness hid her soul from the world. Emotionally exhausted, she wept until she couldn't weep any more. She drifted asleep. The horse stood still—like a mounted horse at a salute during a funeral procession. Raindrops woke her and the horse nickered when he felt her movement on his back.

She reached her arm down and rubbed his neck in a consoling way and whispered, "Hey, buddy. I'm here. I'm not going to let you go."

The raindrops came more rapidly. She sat up, and Traeh shook his head, trying to keep the rain from running into his ears.

"Okay, buddy. Let's get you out of the rain."

She turned the horse around and slowly walked him back to the barn. As she got closer to the barn, she was glad to see the party lights were off, and all she could hear was the rain. Everybody had gone home. It was just her and Cole's horse. That's all she needed—for now.

Chapter 32

Brad couldn't sleep. He sat by the window in his room at the barn. He had told Clara what he saw, and she assured him that Sarah needed to do what she needed to do. She explained that Sarah had gotten a phone call telling her of her aunt's passing, and she was taking care of the girls.

Anxiously, he waited for Sarah's return. The raindrops on his window made it hard for him to see any movements by the corral. Then he saw them. His heart began to pound, and he rushed out the door and down the barn aisle. He didn't know what he would say or do when he reached her, except to hold her in his arms.

"Sarah!"

She focused her eyes forward, not sure if she heard her name. And then she saw Brad.

He cautiously walked up to the horse. "Sarah, it's Brad."

The horse stopped and blew out his breath. Brad rubbed his face and looked up at Sarah. She looked so small and fragile drenched with rain. He reached up and slid her off the horse and held her tightly as the rain continued to fall. She began to sob on his shoulder as he carried her into the barn. The horse followed.

He opened a stall door, led the horse in and unclipped the lead rope. Then he took Sarah to his room and laid her on the couch. Grabbing some towels from the bathroom he wrapped them around her shaking body.

She whispered, "Thanks."

He quickly brought her a shirt and a pair of sweats and offered her to change while he went to check on the horse. He told her he would put her clothes in the dryer. She nodded her head in agreement.

The horse was eager to see Brad with hay in his hand. Brad opened the stall door and tossed the hay on the ground. He then took the towel he had and wiped the excess rain off the horse's back. Before he left he patted the horse's neck and thanked him for taking good care of Sarah.

She sat on the couch in Brad's plaid shirt and sweats. With her knees drawn up into her chest, she wrapped her arms around them. The soft feel and smell of him through his shirt was comforting. She lifted a smile at him when he walked in the room. "How is he?"

"He's fine. I gave him some hay and wiped him down." He saw her pile of wet clothes on the floor next to her and chills ran through him. "Hey, I'm going to get out of these wet clothes, then I'll put your clothes in the dryer with mine. Do you need anything right now?"

She shook her head, and the tears began running down her face again. She was touched by his kindness, but at the same time feeling sorry for herself—he wasn't hers. He was with another girl now, the one he hugged earlier.

Brad came back in the room carrying two cups of hot chocolate. He handed her one.

Her eyes were swollen, but her smile was loving. "Thanks."

She took a sip of the hot chocolate and tears began again.

He took the cup from her and set it next to his. Then he wrapped his arms around her and wiped away her tears. "I'm here for you. Clara told me about your aunt. I'm so sorry."

She reached up and put her arm around his neck and laid her head against his chest. The pounding of his heart beat beating in her ear reminded her she wasn't alone. Closing her eyes and embracing his compassion, she clung to him like a small child until she fell asleep.

***

Sarah woke to the sound of the morning feed cart rattling down the aisle. Sitting up, she looked around and remembered she was in

Brad's room. He stirred, then opened his eyes and gave Sarah a light squeeze when he saw that she was still in his arms.

"Good morning"

She looked at him and smiled. "Good morning. I'm sorry for…"

He cut her off. "No, no. There's nothing to be sorry for. I was glad to be there for you last night."

She smiled. "I better grab my clothes and head over to the kitchen. My girls will be wondering where I am."

Brad nodded. "Okay. Let me get your clothes out of the dryer. Then I'll grab a shower and meet you for breakfast."

He got up and stretched. Sarah watched him and wished that she could wake up beside him every morning. He made her feel safe.

***

Jill was hugging Tara good-bye on the front porch when Sarah walked up. Not wanting to make conversation with them, she lifted her hand and waved.

Once she got in the kitchen she was greeted by Clara's long hug, and was reassured that her girls were okay. "The girls are still asleep. I thought I would come and make them some pancakes. Joe said he would bring them down when they wake up. How are you doing?"

Before she could respond Jill walked into the room and hugged her. She was there to help Clara make the crew's breakfast.

"Clara filled me in on your aunt's passing. I'm sorry. Are there any family members taking care of her funeral arrangements?"

Sarah shook her head. "No, I came from an estranged family. The nursing home told me I was the only contact person in her file, and she wanted to be cremated. I told them I was out of state and would get there as soon as I could to take care of everything that needed to be done. I owe it to my aunt. She was there for me when I had no one."

The room went quiet, and Jill could see Sarah processing everything she had said. "I think I will grab a cup of coffee and make some phone calls. Either way, I need to make a trip to New York as soon as possible."

Clara reassured her that she would take care of the girls for as long as she needed.

Jill nodded. "I'm really sorry that you lost your aunt."

Everyone was reporting in for breakfast before the day started. It was a perk for the workers to have free breakfast on the work days. Travis liked to stay informed on the progress of the B&B remodeling, and this was a pleasant way of doing it. Clara arranged the pancakes and scrambled eggs on the counter, buffet style.

Brad walked in and looked around for Sarah. Then he sat down by Jill and asked if she had seen her this morning. She told him Sarah was making a phone call to find out more information on her aunt's situation.

The last to arrive in the kitchen were the three girls and Grandpa Joe. He led the morning prayer and they all filled their plates and began to eat.

Jill had the honor of announcing the amount of money they raised. "Okay, are you ready to hear how much we raised last night?"

In unison she heard, "Yes!"

She smiled. "Okay, the total amount was…one thousand and two hundred dollars. This includes the items that were in the silent auction donated from the local merchants and the quilter's club. I think that's pretty good for a small town."

Some of them clapped and then she heard someone ask if they knew who won the wedding quilt that went up for raffle.

"As of late last night the person with the winning ticket hadn't come to claim the quilt. Maybe they went home. But the leader of the quilter club said she would call them to let them know they won the quilt.

***

After breakfast Jill asked Travis if she could talk to him before she left for Chicago. They walked toward the pond, making small talk. Once they got there, they sat on the hillside overlooking the pond.

"So—what did you want to talk to me about?"

Jill smiled. "Well, I've been doing a lot of thinking since we were last together, and after seeing you yesterday on stage with the little girls…something came over me."

Travis's face perked up and he turned his body sideways to look at her. "Yeah! What?"

She could see by his mannerisms that he was hoping to hear that she'd had a change of heart about having children. But that wasn't the case; in fact, it was just the opposite. It confirmed to her that "things" had worked out just as they were meant to be. She was ready to leave, head back to work, and continue building her "Unique One" jewelry line as well.

"The passion I saw in you when you were on stage with all the little kids confirmed to me that you thrive on spending time with children. You have even made a business based on children as your target audience. You really care about them. Each of your dolls carries a positive message to inspire the children who might get one for their own.

I want to tell you that I'm in a good place in life with my career and the business that I'm trying to grow. I want to take a big step here and say I think I'll be okay if we move on with our relationship as friends."

Travis was caught off guard. His heart began to feel heavy. He had not expected to hear Jill say the things she was saying, but he knew she was right.

Flabbergasted though, he stuttered, trying to wrap his head around what he knew all along. She was now confirming it.

"Uh—O–Kay…." Rubbing his neck, he continued, "Are you breaking up with me again? Even though we are not a couple any longer?" For some reason, what she was saying reminded him of the rejection he felt when she broke up with him the first time.

She smiled. "Well, not really. Okay, maybe so. I mean when I gave you the letter on the night of my graduation party I left a small window open for a chance to come back if I had made the wrong choice. But now that our lives have played out over the months while being apart, I feel it's time for me to make it final in my mind. So I'm letting you know that I'm okay with you moving on, too…just not with a girl like Sabrina."

Travis shook his head. Looking at her, he smiled. "Oh, I don't know if I'll ever figure you out." He wrapped his arms around her while looking over the pond and voiced the memories they had made there. Knowing this was the best decision for them, his heart lifted. They finally put a closure on their relationship. He hoped they would remain friends.

Chapter 33

Sarah was sitting on the bus waiting to head to New York City. She felt a little anxious traveling alone, but Clara insisted on watching the girls while she went.

Looking out the window she saw a black truck pull in the parking lot. A surge of excitement bounced in her chest. Brad?

Sitting up taller, she waited to see who it was. *Is it Brad? Did he come to take me to New York? I bet Bobby Sue sent him here so I wouldn't have to go alone. She was not happy with me when I insisted on going by myself by bus.*

Finally, she got a good look at the guy. It wasn't Brad.

Sarah slumped in her seat and scolded herself. *"Really? You thought he would come and carry you off this bus and drive you to New York? Hello? Remember the other girl? He is no longer interested in you. You're on your own.* She shook her head, trying to get this third person out of her thoughts.

***

She rested her head against the headrest still wishing he was the guy in the black truck. But no such luck. The bus driver boarded the bus and made a few announcements before closing the door and starting the bus.

She was off to New York.

Brad was disappointed about not seeing Sarah at breakfast. Clara had told him that she was trying to work things out where her aunt was concerned. Not being able to get her off his mind, he decided to text her. "Hey, I missed seeing you at breakfast. Is there anything I can do for you?"

Her phone dinged. Looking at it she read the text from Brad.

She tapped on her phone thinking of what to type. Then she texted Brad, "Sorry, I had to hurry to the bus terminal to get the next bus out to New York City. I don't know how long I will be there, but I want to thank you for your kindness last night."

Alarms went off in his head when he read her text. *Are you kidding? She's on a bus heading to New York? What? By herself! What is she thinking?* He quickly typed a text back to her. "Where are you now? You shouldn't be going to New York City alone."

She was touched by his concern for her. Then she remembered the other girl at the event. This was her life now. She had to stand on her own. First Cole, and then the only family member she had had any contact with had vanished from her life.

She put her thumb on the keypad and tried to figure out how to respond. She wanted to sound stronger than she really felt. She typed, "I'll be fine. The bus driver just pulled away. I don't know when I'll be back. If you would please reassure the girls that I'm okay and I'll be home shortly, I would appreciate it."

Brad was disappointed. He really wanted to spend time with Sarah and be there for her. The next best thing he could do for her was to spend time with her girls until she got home. He closed his phone and went to look for Clara.

Clara and the girls were in the kitchen looking for a glass bowl. The girls had done what they set out to do. They had won goldfish at the event.

Brad walked in the kitchen and being curious he asked, "What's going on?"

The girls ran toward him with their bags of water and a goldfish in each, trying to talk over each other about how they won them.

He sat down at the table and looked at each bagged fish. Then he asked them to take turns and tell him how they each won the fish and what they named it. Clara smiled and grabbed a chair, too. When they were done with their stories, he offered to take them to a store to buy an aquarium and fish food. Clara agreed to his idea and off they went.

***

Bobby Sue ended a phone conversation just as Greta walked into her office. "Hi Mom. What are you doing?"

She smiled at her daughter. "Hi. I just got off the phone with someone that I met at the last Grande performance. Her name is Cheyenne and she runs a horse therapy program in Wyoming. I asked her some questions on how to go about doing horse therapy for Brad."

"Brad?'

Yes. He asked me the other day if he could do it here. His doctor recommended it to help unlock his hips and keep his back in alignment. Anyway, she offered to stop in. She's coming here for the Quarter Horse Congress event. So pretty soon we will have our first official guest staying at the B&B."

Greta smiled, "Nice. I think that is really cool. I can't wait to meet her and learn more about it."

***

Sarah texted Jill about her aunt's death and told her she was on a bus heading to New York to sign some documents for her aunt's cremation. During their conversation Jill wanted to know where she was going to stay. Sarah had no plans. Everything happened so fast that she hadn't even thought about it. Jill told her she would get in contact with Wanda, the waitress at the diner where Jill and Sarah first met. She had let Jill, Sarah and the girls stay in the room above the diner during a snowstorm.

Sarah was so grateful for her friendship with Jill. Jill was like an angel watching over her. She had never had a friendship with anyone like this one. Even though they didn't do a lot with each other, Sarah felt she would always be there for her.

Jill texted her with the information on how to get in touch with an Uber service to get her around. She said that Wanda would be at the diner to greet her when she arrived. Sarah felt better about traveling in New York alone. She almost felt like she had family waiting on her arrival, which was the opposite. She was only there to put closure on her aunt's life—the only person who had taken her in when she'd had nowhere to go. Now it was her turn to show respect to her aunt and see to her final request to be cremated.

Wanda waved at her when she walked into the diner. It was crowded. A group of Mennonite girls filled the booths, so she took a seat at the counter. Looking across the counter she saw a framed picture of the time they were stuck in the snowstorm. She smiled. It was a dark time in her life, and even though they were in a winter storm, Jill brought laughter and light into their situation. The girls colored snow friends with food coloring and dressed them with Jill's extra clothes. Then Jill and the girls made snow angels in the snow all around their snow friends.

Next to the picture was another picture of two draft horses, Billy and Bob. They were the team of horses that Travis used to find Jill after the snowstorm. Sarah leaned in closer to the picture to see herself holding one of the horse's faces and resting her head on his jaw. Jill and the girls were in the background standing around the horses petting them. Wanda took these pictures so she could frame them and hang them on the wall. And sure enough, she did.

Before arriving that night at the diner, she saw no future. That was the last weekend she saw Cole. She had nowhere to go except her aunt's house.

Wanda was busy filling orders, but she took a moment to give Sarah a quick hug and whispered. "I'm glad to see you." Then she poured her a glass of water and handed her a menu.

Sarah smiled. As painful as she anticipated this trip to be, she felt a small glimpse of love. Love from the Gunners, who gave them a place to live… from Clara, who bonded with her and her girls, and who was now watching over them while she attended to her aunt's final request… from Jill, her angel friend, who had been there for her even when she didn't know herself what she wanted or needed, had arranged for her to stay at the diner again while in New York City… and now, she noted Brad's unconditional love even though he didn't belong to her. This all brought her full circle from when her life first came crashing down.

As she tried to focus on the menu, she thought she heard a familiar laughter from one of the booths behind her. She paused from looking at the menu. Afraid to turn around, she thought. *What? No—it can't be! What would she be doing here?*

Slowly, she swiveled her stool around just enough to glance at the group of Mennonite girls. There she sat amongst them—Rosa.

Sarah gasped out loud and quickly spun her stool back around, with her hand over her mouth. Taking a deep breath, she swallowed hard as her mind raced back to the last time she saw Rosa. It was with Cole.

Mennonite? Rosa is Mennonite? But…she was wearing jeans and a tee-shirt—not Mennonite garb—at all the rodeos. Why is she wearing this now?

She grabbed her glass of water and downed it. What was going on with her life? Was she being punished for something? Everything was closing in on her. She felt dizzy. She laid her head on the counter then passed out and slid down to the floor.

The Mennonite girls rushed over to her and Rosa yelled for Wanda's help. With the girls shaking her and all the commotion, Sarah came to. Opening her eyes she saw Rosa looking down at her. She blinked her eyes a few times with a few shakes of her head. Then she heard a familiar voice.

"What happened?" Wanda asked as she tried to move in closer to Sarah.

The girls were all talking at once. Sarah sat up, rubbing the side of her head then cradling it in her hands. Wanda asked the girls if they could go back to their seats. She wanted to talk with Sarah. She helped her stand and walked her into her office. She grabbed Sarah some more water and a muffin.

Sarah thanked her and nibbled at the muffin. "I'm sorry."

"Oh, child. There's nothing to be sorry about. I'm just glad you're okay. It's been a long day for you. I'll go fix you something to eat. How about some eggs? It will be light on your stomach."

Sarah nodded. "That would be great."

Wanda headed out the office door when she ran into Rosa. "Oh! Are you ready to check out?"

Rosa smiled. "Yes. But first, is she alright?" She pointed toward Sarah.

Wanda looked back toward Sarah. She saw that she had eaten most of the muffin and she didn't look so pale. "Yes. She had a long travel and after getting something more to eat, she should be fine."

Rosa hesitated, then asked. "Could I speak with her?"

Wanda was surprised with the question, "Uh—yeah, I guess so. I'm going to make her something to eat, so maybe it would be good if someone was sitting with her until I get back."

Rosa spoke first as they made eye contact. "You're Sarah. Right? Cole's wife? You won the barrel racing title last year in Indiana?"

Sarah's breath quivered when she heard Rosa address her as Cole's wife. She was afraid to breathe while trying to understand what was happening at the moment.

Rosa continued, "I was a big fan of yours and your husband's. I had never seen anything before like what you guys did with horses, barrels and bulls. You really impressed me."

Sarah released her breath and stared at nothing. Her heart felt convicted, but to what? Why did she feel so ugly right now? Tears rolled down her cheeks. The sorrow in her heart was more then she could bear—her aunt's death...seeing Cole's horse again and now the mention of his name by Rosa, a Mennonite?

Not looking at Rosa she asked, "Who are you?"

Rosa answered, "My name is Rosa and I met you over a year ago at a rodeo in Indiana. I was staying with my cousins for the summer. You were the first barrel racer I had ever seen. I fell in love with the sport of rodeo so much I tried to attend as many as I could before I returned home to my family."

Staring at Rosa's shoes, she asked. "Can I ask why you are wearing that outfit?"

Rosa sat at an empty seat beside her. "Oh, maybe that's why you don't recognize me. I'm Mennonite."

Sarah looked at her feeling exhausted, but she had to know more. She asked, "But you were wearing jeans and a tee-shirt. Am I right? You and two other girls?"

Rosa blushed and nodded her head. Then she confessed. "Yes. You see, I am a Mennonite. My family's lifestyle is more on the conservative side, but my cousins live an English lifestyle. But still...they are Mennonites. So when I stay with them I wear the English clothing."

Sarah nodded her head. This girl who she thought was after her husband was only an innocent fan. She wasn't a 'Buckle Bunnie' chasing after Cole after all. She was just a girl impressed with the sport of rodeo. Then guilt engulfed her.

Rosa stood. "Hey, listen. I have to go now. I hope you're feeling better. I'll keep you in my prayers."

Sarah stood and touched her arm. "Thank you for sharing your story with me. You'll never know how much it means to me." Then she gave her a smile.

Rosa smiled back at her. As she started to walk away, she stopped and turned back to give Sarah a hug and said, "I'm really sorry about your husband. I prayed for him that night."

Sarah held her tight, once a stranger in the crowd. A person who she saw as wanting to take away her husband. And here Rosa stood hugging her and offering condolences. Tears flooded her eyes and shame filled her heart as she wept in Rosa's arms.

"Rosa, please forgive me. I had you all wrong. Thank you for praying over my husband when I didn't know how." Rosa nodded her head and slipped out of her hold before walking away.

Chapter 34

The girls put their new aquarium in Brad's office. They had talked him into buying a 55-gallon tank for their three tiny goldfish, making sure they had plenty of room to grow.

The three young girls spent lots of time at the horse barn. Greta had offered to give them riding lessons to help fill their time while Sarah was away. Brad attended and watched each lesson attentively. He now wanted to know everything about the horses. Hearing how to cue the horses would make him more comfortable to be around them once therapy started.

The girls brushed the horses and hand-grazed them while sharing with Brad what they wanted to be when they got older. Tessa said she wanted to be like her mama, a famous barrel racer. Elise wanted to be a trick rider, and Aubrey a Grande rodeo drill team rider. He felt close to Sarah while spending time with her girls. He could see her through their different mannerisms. He wondered about Cole, their father. Why wasn't he a part of their lives? Remembering his own inability to produce children made him very sensitive to the thought of these girls without a father. He wondered if Sarah would ever let him fill that role.

***

Travis was standing at the front desk showing Bobby Sue the spreadsheet and how to input data information on overnight guests and run the credit card machine. He had everything set up and ready for their first guest to arrive.

The screen door squeaked opened, and Cheyenne walked in. Travis glanced up to see who it was, and his fingers stopped moving on the keyboard. A smile lifted on his face, and his eyes brightened.

"Hello. Welcome to the Gunner's Bed and Breakfast."

He walked around the counter and reached out his hand to greet her. "I'm Travis, you must be Cheyenne."

She nodded her head. "Yes. Nice to meet you." Then she shook his hand.

Bobby Sue stood back and enjoyed watching Travis's first encounter with Cheyenne. She too, had been smitten with her natural beauty and disposition when she first met her.

Travis turned toward his mom then realized he was still holding Cheyenne's hand. He quickly let go, saying, "Oh. Sorry, hey, um—you know my mom, Bobby Sue..."

Bobby Sue smiled and walked around the counter. "Hello! Welcome! I'm so glad you could come."

Cheyenne reached out to embrace her. Then she let go and said, "Thank You. I'm glad to be here. And..." looking around she marveled at how beautiful the entryway looked. "I love this place. I mean, driving up the driveway and seeing the horses out in the corral made me feel like I'm at home."

Bobby Sue smiled. "Oh, I'm glad to hear it. Well, let's get you signed in. You're our first guest. Travis will watch over me to make sure I have it down pat, checking you in."

They all laughed.

Travis could not let go of his smile as he looked at Cheyenne. He was mesmerized with her beauty, mannerism, smile, voice, and her accent. Not only her fragrance, but also her whole being filled his heart with hope. He had never felt anything like this before. Or the fact that he was sure he wanted to know everything about her, but didn't know where or how to start.

"Travis, why don't you get her luggage and show her which room is hers." Bobby Sue offered. Then she continued as she sensed his willingness to hang around. "And then after lunch we could walk her around the horse facility."

"Okay, sure!"

They walked outside to grab her luggage and met the three girls in the driveway. They were hyped up and talking over each other until Brad caught up with them.

"Hey, girls. Shh, simmer down. You're going to scare our first guest." Attempting to show the girls the proper way to greet a new guest, he held his hand as if greeting Cheyenne.

"Hello, I'm Brad, and you must be Cheyenne."

She laughed. "Yes. I am. Nice to meet you." Then she pointed to each of the girls as she continued. "And you, and you and you."

Travis loved how she included the girls into the greeting. He in turn, introduced the girls. "This is Elise, Tessa, and Aubrey."

Then to the girls: "This is our new horse therapy instructor. She is here on a visit to help Brad make a full recovery from his accident."

Elise looked up at her solemnly and said, "Wow, I wish you would have been able to help my dad when he got hurt."

Tessa put her hands on her shoulders and gave her a little gentle shake. Elise looked at her, and Tessa gave her a stern look.

Elise lowered her head and mumbled. "Well, I do. Then maybe he would still be with us."

Brad and Travis gave a sharp surprised look to each other, and Cheyenne felt the air go still.

Stooping down in front of Elise, she looked into her eyes. "Oh, sweetie. I'm not sure what happened to your Daddy, but I'm not a doctor. I'm here to help guide the horse to strengthen Brad's muscles. I heard that he has done a lot of physical therapy already and is doing remarkably well. Maybe you can be my helper?"

Elise smiled when she heard she could be a helper. Then she looked at Brad for approval. He smiled and nodded his head.

Travis smiled and told them to go wash up for lunch. The girls scurried along with Brad following behind.

Brad could not keep his focus on the conversation during lunch. If what Elise expressed was what he thought it meant, then Cole had somehow died, and they didn't have a father. His heart was heavy. Poor Sarah. He felt an urgency to talk with her. He excused himself from the table and went to his office.

He stared at the fish tank on his table and watched the three goldfish swimming around. He had loved taking the girls shopping for the fish stuff. Tessa had made a list of what they needed for the tank. Elise and Aubrey were most excited about the glass beads they picked out for the bottom of the tank.

Shaking his head, he looked at his watch and saw that it was a little past noon. Then he thought, *what do I say to her? Hey, did your husband die? Maybe I should tell her how I feel about her and let her tell me about her husband when she's ready.*

Bing. Brad looked at his phone. It was Sarah. He smiled as he opened the text.

"Hey, how are the girls?"

"Great. How are you doing?"

Sarah told him. It had been a long day, but she was able to get a lot done with Wanda's help. He questioned her as to who Wanda was. She explained she was the waitress at the diner where Jill and she had first met. The two of them had stayed with her overnight in a room above the diner during the winter storm last year. Even though it was a sad time, Sarah said she was grateful for all her new friends and she'd be lost without them.

He wanted to hear her voice and asked if he could call her later. She said yes, it would be fine. He put his phone away and stared out the window. He saw the girls with Travis and Cheyenne walking toward the barn. He thought to himself that he had better meet up with them for his first therapy session. All he really wanted to do was think about Sarah and learn more about her husband.

***

Brad caught up with everyone as they heard a horse pounding in his stall. The girls ran ahead and stopped at the new horse's stall. Being rambunctious, he nickered and bobbed his head up and down.

Cheyenne giggled, "Oh, now someone wants out of his stall." She looked at Travis for permission to open the stall door.

He grinned and gestured with his hand to go ahead. She opened the door with ease and stared at the horse's eyes. Greeting him in a monotone voice, Cheyenne slowly lifted her hand to his nostrils so that he could smell her. Then he looked down at her hand and smelled her, cautiously.

"What a beautiful boy you are."

He blew out his breath while lowering his head, showing her he welcomed her into his space without any fear.

"Oh, good boy." she said, as she accepted his body language. Then she continued to move her hand over his jaw and down his neck caressing him. She took a step forward and he willingly took a step back. Patting his chest, she turned and looked at Travis.

"Wow. Is this the new horse you were telling me about at lunch?"

Travis smiled. "Yes. He's a pretty awesome horse. Why don't we lead him to the corral while you're working with Brad. Then, if you want, you can ride him later."

The girls chimed in. "Yay!" They hurried to grab his halter and lead rope, fighting over who would do what.

Brad spoke up, "Hey, hey. Tessa, since Elise is going to help Miss Cheyenne, you and Aubrey can help with the horse now.

Cheyenne stepped out of the stall and followed Travis to retrieve the horse for Brad to use for therapy riding.

Chapter 35

It was Sunday morning, and Sarah wished she was home so she could go to church. Ever since she went with Clara and Joe, she felt good in the atmosphere of it all. Strangely, she couldn't believe how she felt like she belonged, and everyone made her feel like they were her friends.

When talking with Brad the other day, he had asked her when she thought she would be back. She had everything done and was ready to order her bus ticket when Wanda asked her if she could stay and help her with a catering job. She was more than happy to help Wanda last night. Wanda had done so much for her, and she wanted to pay her back in any way she could.

After breakfast Sarah decided she would take a walk while listening to her podcast. It was great to learn that she could listen to her church pastor online.

Another great message was delivered from the pastor today. It seemed as though every one of them she heard were meant just for her. They resonated with her situation every time. This one was on God's Timing. He orchestrates everything to fall into place for His purpose to prepare a person for their future. And if we choose to see things as stepping stones and not interference to reach our ultimate destiny we will have a fulfilled life. A life with hope and a future.

It was a beautiful day. The warmth from the sunshine felt good on her face. The birds were chirping and flying back and forth between trees. She decided to keep walking, enjoying the views of New York City. Since her previous times in the city had been very sad, she wanted to leave looking at the beauty it had to offer and not think about her present situation.

Wanda was busy writing up the weekly specials on the chalkboard when she heard the door open to the diner.

She turned around and her eyes brightened at the handsome gentleman who had just walked in.

Her smile was big as she welcomed him and offered him a seat at the counter. Since he was alone she thought he might want some company, and who better than herself, working behind the bar.

"Would you like to see a menu? Or could I start you off with something to drink?" She asked as she was eager to hear his voice.

"Um, no. Actually I'm not here to eat. I was wondering if Sarah Cutter is here?"

Wanda stared at him. She cautiously asked, "Why? And who wants to know?"

The guy smiled with a slight chuckle and explained why he wanted to see her. It had been too long since he had seen her, and he wanted to take her home.

Wanda being Wanda, a hopeless romantic, told him what she knew. "She took off this morning on foot in that direction." She pointed toward the east. He got up quickly and thanked her as he went out the door. Now to find the love of his life—Sarah.

***

Sarah was sitting on a park bench watching the people walk by. There was a group of young dancers who stopped and started dancing. A crowd began to gather. She was entertained with the energetic moves these dancers put into their act as the music played loudly. She felt a tap on her shoulder, and when she turned around she gasped.

"What! What are you doing here?" She then heard the words that she had been longing to hear.

"I came to take you home."

She stood. Feeling very confused, she stuttered, "But—but how did you find me?"

"Well, I prayed. And I asked Wanda at the diner. She directed me in the path that you left on—and here I am."

Shaking her head, she questioned him, "But…what about the other girl?"

Brad reached for her and pulled her into his embrace. "Come here. There is no other girl. I can explain everything. Let's get out of here, and go where it's quieter so we can talk."

Sarah hung onto him. They walked as a couple with their arms around each other to another park bench. It was much quieter and there were fewer people walking by.

She was still in awe of his coming to get her.

Then she asked, "So, how—why—why are you in New York City?"

He smiled. "I came to bring you home. I couldn't stand the thought of you riding a bus back home. Besides, the girls miss you and so do I."

She smiled. She couldn't believe what she was hearing. Then she heard the jingle and rattle of a horse and carriage. She looked up to see Billy and Bob pulling a white carriage.

Edwin and his wife Annabelle came strolling up to a halt, and asked them if they would like to see New York in style.

Brad immediately jumped up and grabbed Sarah's hand and confirmed his answer. "Yes ma'am."

Edwin stepped down from the carriage and assisted Sarah into the back of the carriage. Brad followed behind her.

Sarah felt like Cinderella being whisked off with her handsome prince.

They sat in awe of each other as they traveled through the streets of New York City. No words were needed. Their smiles, the gentle squeeze of his arm around her as she laid her head on his chest…with the touch of her hand resting on his thigh…this was the language of love they shared as they rode through the park.

Edwin drove the team of horses up to the diner. Wanda came running out taking pictures. She then walked up to Billy and Bob and gave them a big rub on their faces. Then she saw Sarah and her handsome friend sitting in the carriage.

Sarah giggled and waved at her. "Hi. I'm back."

Wanda's jaw dropped. "What? This is unbelievable! Now, I must get a picture of this exciting moment." She took her phone and clicked away, and continued to say, "Now this picture is definitely going on the diner's wall."

Everyone laughed. Then Edwin helped Sarah out of the back of the carriage and Brad followed. They hugged each other and then Brad tipped Edwin and thanked Annabelle while Sarah hugged Billy and Bob.

As they drove off, Sarah noticed the wooden sign hanging where a license plate would hang on their carriage. It read. "Proverbs 17:22."

Wanda couldn't wrap her head around the fact of the draft horses making an appearance twice at the diner. She was going to have to think about adding a hitching post in the parking lot and maybe even adding them as an attraction to the diner. She already decided their picture was going on the wall next to their other one. They made good conversation pieces for the customers.

Chapter 36

Brad and Sarah waved at Wanda as they drove off. Sarah was filled with so many happy emotions that she couldn't stop smiling. Coming back to New York City to fulfill her aunt's final request was actually healing to her. It had been way too long since she felt peace, hope, and now joy in her heart. Wanting Brad more than ever, she wanted to share everything about herself to him. She didn't want anything to be between them if they were going to be a couple.

With a gentle voice. Sarah asked, "Hey, can I share something with you?"

He saw she was more composed than when they first took off. "Uh, sure. What's on your mind?"

"I learned something about myself while in New York," she said.

He took a longer look at her this time. "Yeah?"

"Well…let me start back when I started going to church with Clara and Joe. I was not brought up in church nor did anyone ever try to teach me about church, Jesus or God. The closest I had ever come to singing gospel music was when they played the National Anthem at the start of each rodeo. I do remember seeing my husband, Cole, get down on one knee, remove his hat and bow his head in it before each bull riding session. And after a successful ride he would kiss his finger and point it up to the sky. So—I wanted to believe he was a believer. We lived a fast paced life, having babies, and running the rodeo circuit. We never talked deeply about anything. We lived from one rodeo to another."

Brad had been very inquisitive about her life with Cole and was surprised that she was talking about him now. He looked at her with an acknowledging smile and nodded his head. He wanted to hear more.

She let out a deep breath and looked out her side window. She continued, "So, I want you to know that I took a soul searching walk and after I attended my first church service, I now believe in Jesus. And I have started a relationship with Him by talking to Him every day."

Brad reached over and unfastened her seatbelt. Then he pulled her closer to him on the bench seat. He put his arm around her shoulders and gave her a one-arm hug as he praised her. "That's awesome!"

She smiled and fastened the middle seatbelt, then said, "Yeah. Since then, I have been able to feel good emotions and not be consumed by sad ones. I am able to have hope for a future. Before, I was just walking day to day, making do with the things I had to do in order to wake up another day. If it weren't for my girls, Jill and the Gunner family I don't know if I would have survived."

They drove in silence for a while. Then Brad wanted to clarify his relationship with Tara.

"I want to let you know that my relationship with 'the other girl', Tara, is a platonic friendship. She and I did a few college plays together and, yes, I knew she wanted more out of our friendship than I wanted, and I led her to believe that it could be. But since then I have apologized to her for leading her on. That is why you saw us hugging at the event. I came clear to her about my past feelings, and apologized for hurting her."

Sarah stared straight ahead, watching the road. Resting her head on his shoulder, she was trying to accept all that he shared with her.

***

Travis and Cheyenne had offered to entertain the girls while Brad drove to New York to pick up Sarah. The air was cooling down as the fall weather was pushing in. The girls wanted a campfire with all the 'fixins.' Their plans were to sit around the fire until Brad brought their mama home.

Travis, Cheyenne and the girls gathered firewood and loaded it in the back of the ATV.

They drove by Clara pulling a wagon full of goodies from the kitchen to the picnic table. The girls were screaming and waving their arms up high. They were having the time of their lives.

Travis stopped at the picnic table and pulled up the parking brake. He instructed the girls to put their work gloves on and carry the firewood over to the fire ring.

Bo and Bobby Sue were swinging on the porch swing watching while recovering from the fundraiser.

Bobby Sue leaned in toward Bo and asked, "Do you see that?" She pointed in the direction of Travis.

Bo smiled as he looked over to see Travis instructing the girls on how to carry the firewood while Cheyenne was helping Clara put a tablecloth on the picnic table.

Bobby Sue continued, "Doesn't Travis look happy?"

Nodding, Bo answered, "Yes he does. He's been different ever since Cheyenne came. You don't suppose it's because of her now, do ya?"

Bobby Sue smiled, "I do know it's because of her. He has never been so up about another girl like he is with her. For instance, do you know what he did earlier this morning? He tacked up two horses and took Cheyenne on a ride around the property before the girls got up. He's not one to get up at the break of dawn to ride a horse."

Bo questioned her. "Now, how do you know all of this?"

She answered, "My mom told me. She said that he even took a thermos full of coffee and some muffins, too. I wonder where they stopped for their morning coffee?"

Bo shook his head. "You're a hopeless romantic. Don't try to read too much into it. Besides, she lives in Wyoming."

They started laughing until they heard someone screaming. They looked up to see Cheyenne running around the picnic table yelling, "Get it away from me!" Travis took his hat off and was swinging it in the air. She apparently was afraid of a wasp or a yellow jacket. They continued to watch the scene play out. He finally swapped his hat down on the table and flicked it off. Then he put his hat back on and walked toward Cheyenne. He put his arm around her shoulders and walked her back to the table to reassure her that whatever it was, it was dead.

With a big smile. Bobby Sue pushed off with her foot to make the porch swing go higher.

Chapter 37

Brad pulled off at a roadside rest where there were food trucks selling sandwiches for a fundraiser. Stretching as he got out of the truck, he checked their surroundings. He pointed to a big oak tree with a picnic table under it and asked Sarah if she wanted to grab something to eat and sit there. She agreed; she wanted time to tell him more about Cole. It was time to share his story and use it as part of her healing.

"Brad, this gyro is so big! I don't think I can eat it all."

He smiled, "Okay, hand it over. Can't waste a good thing."

She passed it over to him, then took a drink. Looking around, she watched different types of vehicles and people come and go, wondering if any of them had their own sad story. They all seemed to be in such a hurry. Maybe some of them were like her, living from one event to another, not noticing the small blessings that go with them.

"Thank you for picking me up. This is so much better than riding on a bus."

He frowned, "Is that the only reason you're thankful—for me saving you from a bus ride?"

She smiled then reached over and laid her hand on his forearm. "No! I wouldn't have wanted anyone else to come and get me. I love this time we're having, getting to know each other better."

She squeezed his arm and positioned herself to face the back of the property. She didn't want any distractions while sharing her history with Cole. At the back of the property was a row of large pine trees. Looking at them gave her courage, reminding herself of her recent soul-searching walk. Nature seemed to speak to her. The forever pine tree seemed to breathe life into her somehow, giving her hope of a future with Brad. She felt a heaviness to share her past with him and the dark hole that was once in her.

Brad finished her sandwich and tossed their trash in the trash can. When he returned to the table, he could see that she was composing her thoughts. He sat close and rubbed her back. She looked at him with a smile, then closed her eyes and inhaled deeply. He sat still, watching her closely.

She slowly and gently exhaled. It was time. She turned toward him and held his hand, stroking it gently. She looked into his dark brown eyes that seemed to invite her into his soul. She felt safe with him. She was ready to let go and move forward with God's guidance.

"I'm ready to share my husband's story with you."

Brad swallowed hard. He sensed this would be hard for her, and wanted to give her an "out" if she really didn't think she was ready to do so. "Okay. Only if you really want to."

Nodding her head, she continued. "Yes, I am. You see… Cole had an underlying health condition that we knew nothing about. Or I should say I knew nothing about it until after the autopsy report. I'm not sure if he knew about it or not. We never talked deeply about things. He had a ballooned area in his aortic vessel.

Brad scrunched his forehead and dropped his eyes from her stare.

She cleared her throat and tears welled up in her eyes. She glanced at her forever evergreens and tried to gain courage to speak out loud. Then she looked at Brad. He gave her a small nod to encourage her to go on.

She tried to put on a brave smile, but it failed. Her lips began to quiver, and she had a flash back to the night it all happened.

"You've got this honey! Woohoo," she yelled, as she sat on her barrel horse just outside the arena where the bull riders were competing for the final round. Her horse could feel her excitement and was prancing around. Holding the reins in one hand while fist pumping the air with the other, she was ready for Cole to win the final round. This would put him as the number one all-around bull rider for the year. The money he would win would give them a down payment on a place to call their own. They had lived out of a horse trailer that had living quarters ever since they had married.

Now that their third child had come along, it was their plan to find a real home.

Cole came out of the chute riding the fiercest bull of the night. The crowd stood and cheered him on. He rode that bull with stout maneuvers, like a champ—and a champ he was. The eight-second bell sounded over the PA system. That's when everything seemed to happen in slow motion

Cole released his hand and positioned his body to do a flying dismount. Just as he did, the bull thrust his body up. He reared and came back down hard, throwing Cole forward. The horn of his saddle punched Cole in the lower part of the chest. He went limp. The ballooned area in his aortic vessel had burst.

Sarah continued, seeing the next scene play out in her head.

She yelled. "Nooooo!" She slid off her horse, Black Thunder, and ran into the arena. This was not his first fall, but this was the first time she felt a knife in her heart when he hit the ground.

She stumbled as she ran to him. The crowd noticed an almost deftness in her movements, but she could only hear her heartbeat pounding in her ears. She felt like she couldn't run fast enough to be by his side. Flashes of when they first met—riding in wide open fields together, their kiss at the altar, their first child, then their second and third childbirths flashed in her head. She wanted to get to him, to hold him, to keep him from leaving her.

The medic crew was circled around him when she finally got to him. She stared at them and, when they shook their heads, knew she had lost him. He was gone.

Brad pulled her into a bear hug as she cried. Tears welled in his own eyes as he held her. She lifted her head and grabbed a napkin to blow her nose. She drew a deep breath. She knew she had to tell him everything.

In denial, she shook her head. The crowd had gathered around them. The rodeo crew tried to hold them back. Sarah fell down on his body crying profusely. "Someone please help him. Please." She looked up and saw Rosa on her knees. She was praying.

The emergency squad drove into the arena with more medical assistance, and hurried to him. They asked her to step back so they could try to revive him. But they couldn't. They moved him to the stretcher and laid a sheet over his body. Sarah was in shock as she watched them load him into the squad. The crowd went silent. Her world went black.

Brad couldn't hold back the tears. He cradled her tightly in his arms. "I'm SO sorry."

They stayed in each other's embrace until they couldn't cry any longer.

Sarah looked at Brad and asked, "Why did God take him from us?"

Brad tried to gain composure before he answered her. "Sarah, I don't know why Cole's story ended the way it did. We have no control over how our lives will end. But what I believe is that God doesn't take; He receives. His loving arms are always wide open. It sounds like Cole ended his life doing what he loved. He was a champion bull rider. He left instantly and without pain."

Sarah looked back at the row of pine trees as she replayed in her mind what Brad had said. "God doesn't take—He receives." She felt more at peace with that thought. And she was no longer angry for the loss of Cole.

Out of the corner of her eye she noticed a white puppy sleeping under one of the trees.

"Brad! Do you see that?" She pointed at the puppy.

Brad looked at where she was pointing. "It's a puppy. I wonder where its mommy is?"

Sarah immediately got up and went to the puppy. It lifted its head and yawned. Then it got up and tried to climb on her, all the while yipping and licking her. She smiled and laughed as she cuddled it.

Brad watched and listened at her joyful laughter. He went to the security guard and asked if he knew who the puppy belonged to. The guard told him all he knew was that it had been hanging around there for a few days. He had been throwing him some scraps whenever he was on duty.

Brad walked toward Sarah and the puppy. When he got close, the puppy ran up to him. He bent down and gave the puppy a rub, and looked for a collar. "Hey, little fella. Do you need a home?"

Sarah watched him play with it. She was all smiles. She felt a relief from within. She was glad that Brad now knew about Cole. No more denial, hiding from reality past. Now she could hold onto the thought of God's receiving the best bull rider ever.

Chapter 38

The girls were having fun roasting marshmallows around the fire. Cheyenne was very organized. She had two graham cracker squares laid on a napkin with a square of chocolate on top of them. When the girls would scream, "Hurry. Blow it out," She knew it was time to sandwich the melting marshmallows.

"Okay, put it here." She would help them place the burnt marshmallow on top of the chocolate and use the graham crackers to pull it off the stick.

Travis got a text from Sarah with their arrival time. He had another 45 minutes to kill before he could have alone time with Cheyenne. He liked everything about her. She was great with the girls. Didn't whine about getting her hands dirty either. He thought he would challenge her, though, with catching frogs at night with a flashlight and their hands only

"Okay kids, do you know what time it is?" Travis questioned them.

"No. What?" They answered in unison.

He stood holding a bag. Then he asked them to put their hand in the bag and pull one item out of it. They were fighting over who got to go first. After they each had a flashlight they wanted to know what they were going to do with it. He told them they were going to hunt frogs with a flashlight. Aubrey seemed a little unsure about the night, so Travis told her she could be his helper. He was going to carry the bucket to put the frogs in. Then they would bring them back to the campfire to show their mommy.

She smiled. "Mommy will be here?"

Travis picked her up. "Yes, mommy is almost home. So let's go get her a frog." They all hopped in the ATV and headed toward the pond. While they were a great distance from the water, Travis turned the ATV off. He whispered, "Okay girls, turn your flashlights on. Remember we have to walk very quietly, and when you see a frog you can't scream. If they hear us they will jump into the water and go under. Then we won't be able to catch them."

The girls giggled and aimed their flashlights into each other's faces. Aubrey clung to Travis's neck when he lifted her up, and carried the bucket with the other hand. Her job was to aim her flashlight at the ground so he could see where to walk. Cheyenne had to rely on Tessa and Elise to shine their lights for her to see.

Once they reached the pond, Travis held his arm out to signal the girls to stop. Then he scrunched down with Aubrey and stood her on the ground. He took her flashlight and pointed it at a sleeping frog on the edge of the pond.

You could hear the girls gasp. All the flashlights were on that one frog. Travis laid his flashlight down and, with a quick motion, he leaped forward with both hands and scooped up the frog. The girls screamed. The frog made a squelch sound and squirted poop out the other end. Travis quickly laid the frog in the bucket so the girls could watch him. Then he swished his hands in the pond to clean them off.

"Okay, girls, let's take him back to the campfire so we can show your mama when she gets home."

Cheyenne was quite impressed with his frog catching skills. She liked a guy who wasn't afraid to get his hands dirty. And she liked the fact that he was at ease around children.

Clara, Joe, Bobby Sue and Bo hurried out of the B&B when they saw Brad's truck pull in. They took turns embracing Sarah and shaking Brad's hand.

Clara spoke first. "It's good to have you home."

She smiled. "It's good to be at a place I can call home. Where are the girls?"

Bobby Sue told her they would be back soon. They were with Travis and Cheyenne.

Brad could hardly wait to see the girls and show them the surprise they brought. Then he saw the ATV headlights.

When the headlights came around the corner of the B&B, the girls could see Sarah and Brad waving at them from the campfire. They started screaming, "They're here! Mama is home!"

Once Travis stopped the ATV they ran to their mama with lots of hugs and kisses. This was the first time they had ever been separated. They were so happy that they started crying.

Sarah teared up. Not because she was sad, but because she had never felt so much love in one moment. First, from Brad, for all that he did for her during this time, then Clara and the whole Gunner family. And seeing her girls again made her value herself more as being privileged to have her three daughters. She would always have a part of Cole with her through his children.

Travis carried the bucket with the frog in it and set it in front of Sarah. The girls were talking all at once, trying to tell her how they caught the frog and wanted her to hold it. She talked them out of her holding it by telling them they should let it go back to its home because she had a surprise for them that would need lots of attention.

Brad stood at his truck waiting for Sarah's cue. She gave a sharp whistle, and he knew it was time. He opened his truck door, and out flew the little white puppy they had found.

The girls were ecstatic when they saw the puppy running toward them. They ran toward the pup and sat down so it could jump on them and lick each one of them. Then they started chasing it, and it would chase them back. They played with the puppy nonstop for half an hour. Then the puppy found Sarah and whined. Sarah told the girls that it was late, and the puppy was tired. It was time to turn in. They were all for going to bed when they thought the puppy was going to sleep with them. But Brad broke the news to them that the puppy had to sleep with him at the barn.

Travis asked Cheyenne if she would like to walk to the pond and take the frog back. Without hesitation she agreed. They said their goodnights to everyone and left on foot to the pond. Without a flashlight the full moon lit their path, giving an intimate feel to their surroundings. They could hear the bull frogs croaking and the crickets chirping as their feet swished through the dew on the grass

Travis spoke first. "Hey, thanks for all you did today. You were really good with the girls. And, wow, you are a natural with horses, too." He sensed her smile when she purred a pleasant sound of humility.

"You're welcome. It felt really good being around those little girls. I can't wait to start a family of my own. As for horses, well, I've been around them all my life. My mom was a horse breeder and trainer. We raised old foundation quarter horse paints. We actually have a few of her mares and a stallion still on our farm."

"Really? So does your mom still breed horses?"

He could hear her inhale—then exhale before she answered. "No. She is no longer with us. It's just me and my dad. She passed away a few years ago."

Travis felt bad for asking about her mom. He stumbled for the right words to say, "Oh Chy...I'm so sorry. I didn't know. I wouldn't have asked if I had known..."

She wrapped her hand around his upper arm and leaned in as they continued to walk. Softly, she spoke, "It's okay. You didn't know. Besides, I have a lot of good memories of her. She taught me everything I know about horses."

She felt like she had known Travis for more than a week. She was comfortable with him, and she liked the fact that he had just called her Chy. She continued, "Maybe I'll share them with you, someday."

He liked the fact that she didn't let go of his arm when she took hold of it as she tried to comfort him with her words.

He whispered, "I would like that."

They continued to walk, listening to the night sounds of nature until they reached the pond and released the frog.

Cheyenne felt a new awareness about herself as they stood beside each other in the moonlight. The fresh crisp breeze seemed to waken her senses. She could smell Travis's cologne and liked the feel of his closeness. After her mom had died suddenly from a brain aneurysm, Cheyenne had taken over the family business. Breeding, working with the foals, giving them lots of ground handling, marketing them for purchase, running the therapy program, and riding lessons. Her only social time was on Sundays when she would attend her father's church. He was a long-standing pastor at the local church, and they would spend Sundays together. She looked forward to eating lunch together after church. It was father-daughter time to catch up with each other. Other than Sundays at church, she didn't spend much time with others socially because she had so many business responsibilities.

Out of nowhere she blurted out an invitation to Travis. "Hey, would you like to go back to Wyoming with me to meet my dad and see our operation?" She paused to hear his response and was glad that it was dark out, because she didn't know why she impulsively just asked him to go home with her. It was like her emotions took over. She had not had a serious relationship or for that matter, dated anyone.

As she was growing up her family were active missionaries and self employed. She felt she had a balanced life of serving others and learning to be self motivated in creating a family business. But something new was stirring in her since she met Travis. He felt like a missing piece of her, and she couldn't stand the thought of leaving him and going back home.

Travis was elated with her invitation. He hadn't been looking for a relationship. But the first time he laid eyes on her, he knew in his heart she was the one. And he never wanted to let go of that feeling.

"Really!?" He wanted a confirmation on what he just heard her ask of him.

She smiled broadly and nodded her head to confirm her offer.

Right then, Travis felt it. He confirmed to himself. Someday— he was going to marry this girl.

"Um—yeah sure. I would love to!"

The moonlight was shining on her face; she looked so radiant, like an angel. An angel meant just for him. He moved in closer to her, and like two magnets drawn together, it was genuine. Gently, he put his arms around her and kissed her passionately.

Chapter 39

There was so much electrifying joy in the air the next morning. Everyone who gathered around the table was in a good place in their lives.

Travis told them that he would be taking some time off to travel to Wyoming with Cheyenne. Then, he asked Brad if he would help oversee the Bed and Breakfast while he was gone. Brad assured him that he was qualified for the job.

Sarah had made peace within her soul, and had learned to accept the things she couldn't understand or change in her past. Accepting God as her personal Savior and having a relationship with Him had given her an awareness of the blessings He had given her during her darkest times.

Like the timing of meeting Jill, after having been snowed in at the diner, it was through Jill's passion of loving others that gave her the desire to have what she was giving. At the time she hadn't known how to get it.

Then the timing, when the aunt she had been living with had been moved to a nursing home when her house went into foreclosure, leaving her with no home and forcing her to find a new place. This change resulted in her finding the Gunner's Bed and Breakfast. They loved on her and her children with unconditional love. They asked no questions of her or her situation and gave her a job and a place to live with her girls.

Clara and Joe introduced her to church. That's when the healing started. The hurt, pain, and emptiness within were replaced with love from accepting and learning of God and His unconditional love.

When reacquainted with Cole's horse, she thought about how God led Bobby Sue to the horse, Traeh, and put the desire on Bobby Sue's heart to bring him to the Gunner's equestrian center. She had no doubt it was meant for her. To again have the horse that made Cole who he was there with her somehow helped release the loss of him.

The death of her aunt was the final breaking point in her life. But, going back to New York to honor her Aunt's final wishes, brought her more healing moments. It led her to begin breaking down the walls that she had thought would protect her heart from more pain. As the walls came down, she felt the desire to live and love again.

Running into Rosa, she now knows, wasn't a coincidence. God had orchestrated everything in His timing for all good purposes. After seeing Rosa again, she learned not to judge others by what you think, but to take time to learn about them. Don't judge outward appearances...look at others through the eyes of Jesus. His greatest command is to love one another.

Rosa was loving them by praying at the time of her husband's tragic accident. She hadn't let that register then, but it may have helped unknowingly to comfort her.

She was most thankful to learn that Brad was patiently waiting for her. When she opened up to him about her past and wanting to move on with her life, she was overwhelmed with what God had allowed to happen. She wanted to explore a relationship with Brad, a man who loved her and her three girls.

After breakfast they all stood on the front porch and waved goodbye to Travis and Cheyenne. Bo put his arm around Bobby Sue when he heard her sniffle. Her instincts were right about the natural attraction between Travis and Cheyenne. Tears of joy filled her eyes as she blew a kiss goodbye to her firstborn. She hoped they would come back wanting to be married. Someday.

Book club questions for discussion.   *Chapters 28-39*

❖ *What are your thoughts about the announcement of the etching on the career doll's right foot? Do you think it was a way for Travis to show his acceptance of Jill's decision to choose career over love?*

❖ *Read Titus 2 from the Bible. It talks about passing down Christian values from generation to generation. The grandparent dolls that Clara and Joe represented were created to remind us of their responsibilities in the family. Who has been your Titus person in directing you to stay on the right path of life?*

❖ *Have you been in a relationship where you were invested in it more than the other person? Did it end well, like Brad's and Tara's did during their lunch date?*

❖ *In Chapter 31, Sarah felt God brought Cole's horse to her as a way of comforting her when she found out she lost another person that she loved—her aunt. Have you experienced something or has someone been put in your life at the right time to help comfort you?*

❖ *What's your thought on Brad's point of view when Sarah asked him why God took Cole from them? His response was —God doesn't take, He receives. His loving arms are always wide open.*

Book club questions for discussion.   *Chapters 28-39*

❖ *Sarah has been able to see life through the lens of John 15:17 (This is My command: Love each other.) since she has been actively attending church and learning scriptures. In Chapter 39 she reflects over the many blessings in her life after she accepted God as her personal Savior and began developing a relationship with Him. Would you agree that by being an active Christian your eyes are more sensitive to the many blessings that we receive?*

❖ *Both Travis and Cheyenne felt a natural attraction and were immediately drawn toward each other. They had the same values and qualities of a partner they were looking for. Do you believe in love at first sight?*

***

Thank you for taking time to read my second book in the

New Beginnings Series.

I hope it has inspired you in a special way. I would love to connect with you and hear your thoughts about the book.

You can contact me at:

Authorsusanschmelzer@aol.com

(Facebook) Author Susan Schmelzer

The theme of New Beginnings Series was based on
Jesus' teaching in John 15:16, 17
"You did not choose Me, but I chose you and
appointed you to
go and bear fruit—fruit that will last. Then the Father
will give
you whatever you ask in My Name. This is My
command:
Love each other." (NIV)

Salvation is offered as a gift to us by God. The way to receive it is believing, accepting who Jesus is, and asking Him into your heart.

Romans 10:8-10 But what does it say? "The Word is near you, It is in your mouth and in your heart," that is, the Word of faith we are proclaiming.
That if you confess with your mouth, "Jesus is Lord," and believe in your heart that God raised Him from the dead, you will be saved. For it is with your heart that you believe and are justified, and it is with your mouth that you confess and are saved.

Living out the knowledge of Scriptures and believing in It—is living by faith.

Hebrews 11:1 "Faith is being sure of what we hope for and certain of what we do not see."